PRAIRIE STARPORT
Stories in Celebration of Candas Jane Dorsey

Rhonda Parrish

Poise and Pen Publishing

EDMONTON, ALBERTA

www.poiseandpen.com

Front cover design by James of GoOnWrite.com
Back cover design by Jonathan C. Parrish featuring art by Alexandrea Flynn and Annalise Glinker

Book Layout based on one © 2014 BookDesignTemplates.com

Prairie Starport/ Rhonda Parrish.—1st ed.
ISBN 978-1-988233-38-3 (Physical)
ISBN 978-1-988233-39-0 (Electronic)

For Candas

CONTENTS

INTRODUCTION

"There comes a time when you need to stop pretending that you're still an apprentice and admit that maybe you know some things."

Candas and I were driving home after consuming an obscene amount of sushi and talking about work, and then she said that and *poof* blew my mind. She was right—I had been hiding behind the 'I'm still learning' shield and as terrifying as it was, perhaps it was time I admit to maybe knowing some things. Maybe.

That was just one of many times Candas has said or done something to shift my perspective and teach me about myself, my writing, this industry or the world in general, but that was the specific incident that inspired this collection. See, several months after that conversation I was talking with Greg Bechtel and recounted what Candas had said. He laughed. "She told me pretty much the same thing," he said.

And that got me thinking.

Over the years Candas must have helped, taught, guided and inspired hundreds of people in thousands of ways. She deserved something by way of a thank you.

When I approached her partner, Timothy Anderson, to see if he had any suggestions he said, "My feeling is that it might have to include literature..." and I said, "Oooh! I do anthologies—that is what I do. What if I compiled an anthology that was "Stories in celebration of Candas Dorsey". No acceptances or rejections—we just invite people to send us stuff then I put them together and publish it."

And voila!

This right here? This is the result of that. Of me opening up the door and saying, "If you want to contribute something to this anthology in appreciate of Candas and her work, send it to me."

Originally I'd assumed it would be a collection of fiction, but it very quickly became apparent that not only did non-fiction writers want to contribute but artists also. The result is a fun mix of genres, styles and mediums that I hope will make Candas proud.

Rather than divide this book into separate sections for fiction and non-fiction I've mixed them together. I was careful to make sure I gave Candas the last word, though. I think she'll like that.

Rhonda Parrish
Edmonton
3/14/2018

SLOUGH

Nothing about Alberta bulls is going to inspire a Hemingway, nothing about our fishermen either. The 4-H Club teaches you to care for, and then not care for, a cow. Fishing means a couple of uncles in a shack on the ice in good spirits they brought from home, luring whitefish up to a hole. All the adults talk about is the price of oil, the price of grain, and the price of beer.

Closest we get to poetry is the second half of the sermon, when Reverend Willis riffs on free grace and how being bound to the earth does not mean we are bound to original sin. Nice to know that none of our sin has to be from the time of birth. We can build it up slowly, architects of our own need for redemption.

My folks never said anything good about the Church of the Nazarene over to Caroline. But they still sent me there, squished into the back seat of the Abbotts' rusty car that every other teen would have known the make of. I wanted to ride my bike, but my mother said she wasn't going to have me ruining my Sunday-go-to-meeting clothes, and the logging trucks couldn't be trusted. "They jack-knife, you know."

Everyone at church was intense. They noticed if you didn't look like you were paying attention during the sermon, and while it wasn't a sin for a kid to be bored, it was a sign that Satan could be tempting them.

That Mother's Day we were so busy waiting for Satan to play his hand that the girl in yellow gingham took us by surprise. She walked in like she owned the place. Didn't talk to anyone, just sat on the left end of the Abbotts' pew. Which meant she was sitting where I usually sat, and the Abbotts were habitual, like anyone with livestock, and they were not going to sit anywhere else. So I had to sit beside gingham girl and try to keep my mind on the service instead of trying to remember which of the four quadrants of the Land of Oz had everything yellow and did Dorothy Gale ever go there in her gingham dress and did it change colour. We had the books. Pretty sure the Winkies were yellow.

She sang all the hymns, but maybe not the tune. After the service, she got on a bike handpainted with bluebells and pedalled unevenly down the pebbly road until she couldn't be seen anymore. So the Abbotts dropped me home and I told my parents they should let me ride my bike to church, because This Girl. Sunday dinner was then my mother's monologue about who the girl might be and what bad parents she must have to let her bike on these roads alone. "They jack-knife, you know," was all I said.

My dad didn't laugh. He gave me that don't-get-smart-with-your-mother look and got up from the table. "If she offers you marijuana, say no politely," he said.

The next week she told me her name was Shell, short for Seashell, and her parents were hippies and they wanted to have sex on Sunday mornings so she came to church to give them some privacy because the library wasn't open. When she said that, I felt a click, a lock snicking shut on knowledge that cannot be unhooked from Sunday mornings. Libraries are not open; parents have sex.

Every Sunday was like that. Shell would arrive, always in the same dress, and she would say something that made the world more real. I asked if her parents walked around naked, and she said there were too many blackflies for that. Sometimes inside, but not since she started getting her period. Besides, hippies and nudists were not mutually inclusive variables. She told me all about that, and that she was really fourteen. Snick.

At the end of June, my parents said I could stay home on Sundays for the summer. I told them I would keep going to church so they could have time for sex. My dad invited me out to the porch for a talk.

The mosquitoes and blackflies were bad. He didn't look at me, but there wasn't anyone else he could be talking to. "No need for the sex talk," he said, "but I promised your mother to have a word with you, so look different when you go inside. And if this girl offers you anything…"

"I promise to think of Nancy Reagan."

Truth? They both inhabited an uncanny valley, the dead First Lady and the living Shell. One Sunday Shell showed me her new rose gold chain with a small gold-plated shell dangling from it. "Combination fifteenth birthday and a good early harvest," she said. The rose gold didn't really go with the yellow gingham, that dress that made her look so much younger. And nothing that grows naturally here is ready for harvest except asparagus, and how much asparagus would it take to buy a gold necklace?

"What we grow is different from what most people grow," she said. "You smoke it."

None of my business. But when the Abbotts went away on vacation I was allowed to ride my bike, and then my parents stopped paying attention so I could do it even when they got back. Once we got to the church at the same time and we stayed outside where we could hear but not be seen, where we could trade notes and no-one would hand us a pamphlet about the hell that awaits us. But when the service was over and there was lemonade in the hall, the church ladies looked at us like we had been doing the devil's work. So the next week we met a block away from the church and didn't go at all. We headed for the other side of the highway, because the library was closed, and we picked berries and talked about stuff. She was home-schooled and knew way more about way less.

Then one of my great uncles got sciatica and my mother and father started driving to Sundre a couple of evenings a week, to do whatever needed doing.

That night Shell called "Follow me!" and pedalled fast to beat me over the first rise. We went over a few more before she turned into a gravel road and kept going. I knew she wanted to lead, to be first, so I took my time following the dust. Then I saw the bike leaning against a pole by the side of the road, and past a kind of embankment I could see the back of Shell's head and her shoulders. The light was weakening, so she looked like a cutout stuck into the embankment itself. I clambered over to see what she was staring at.

"It's a slough," I said.

Johnston's slough was nothing to look at during the day, even the ducks didn't bother with it, but as the colour leached from the land-scape the menacing obelisk defied landlogic, seeming to rise.

"Wait."

The wind picked up, stars came out and Shell's necklace caught the last ray of sun as her skin turned gooseflesh in the chill.

Then there they were, dancing lightly, the stars under them, darker than the sky above.

"The only way to go up," she whispered, "is to go in."

"You have to be nuts to think you're going to find anything in Johnston's slough. Leeches, maybe."

Moments later she was in, and physics were upturned as the sound of her travelled faster than the sight of her, the splashes shattering the starport and the ghost of her body moving through the warp.

Then she was standing there, wet, skin and glimmer and I used the lighter she had in her bag to heat them until they dropped, brought life to her corpse by sacrificing a half dozen tiny aliens. The yellow of the lighter flame blinded me to everything but her skin, the gross leeches, the blood running red and dropping black out of the light. My breath unsteady.

"I think that's all," I said, hoping it was true.

"You have to be sure."

"Yes. All I can see."

Then she handed me the pale little leech-shaped wad. A metaphorical apple. She had one too, and she lit it. She barely drew in, then she blew out and the smell was something between burning moss and lilacs just before they open.

She looked at me, not daring me but expecting me.

"It's good," she said. "No chemicals. My folks grow rare tobaccos. They don't give you cancer, but they can take a little getting used to. This one isn't sacred or anything, just different."

So I lit up, because it wasn't marijuana but it still might count as defiling my temple. Whatever changed that night wasn't going to unchange.

A few evenings later I was reading on the porch, wondering if citronella candles annoy humans more than they repel insects, when the pulsing started. The low clouds shivered a jittery unsettled shimmer. Likely over by the Johnston place. Ships come to the prairie starport, I guessed. Citronella not effective on aliens. Snick.

Then coming from the direction of the pulsing, headlights latched onto the road, crawling my way. Car accident? They jack-knife, you know. It was our car, my folks back from Sundre and getting out of the car with the dregs of big blue raspberry slushes and their stained lips.

"Something going on over by Johnston's," Dad said. "Maybe the marijuana growers getting busted."

I didn't look up from my book. "Aliens. There are aliens over there."

Even not looking I could tell Mom was tired and wired on blue sugar. Low impulse control thrusters engaged, Captain.

"I think," a whiff of raspberry acid in the words, "we would have noticed a spaceship."

"The aliens are small. Vampiric. They come from the underside of the starport."

The parental unit shook both heads and trudged inside. Later I will find my father sneaking a toilet bowl cleaner into the tank so the water will turn blue. He has told Mom the slush will continue to be blue all the way through the system.

I told Mom and Dad I would set the house on fire if anyone sang Sixteen Candles.

Then the Abbotts got a new car and the old Sunday beater was in our driveway and the keys were on our kitchen table and my parents were saying this is safer than a bike on these roads and it's a Rambler. They would control how much I drove by rationing a fuel allowance.

Pretending to be embarrassed by my effusive gratitude, or lack thereof, Dad buried himself in the pages of the Sundre Roundup. Mom started unloading the dishwasher, realized the dishes were dirty and put them back.

Dad clucked. "Who did they think would buy rare tobacco in these parts? Can't hardly smoke anywhere anyways. Taxes, too. Price point. Can't blame them for leaving." He passed the paper to Mom, who put it on the counter.

"You'll want to read that," he said to her.

"Maybe later," she said. "Dishes don't do themselves."

"You'll want to read it," he pressed. "Interesting recipe for a jellied salad."

I wanted to call out "Oxymoron!" but when I looked up I saw the secret message pass between them, saw Mom pick up the paper and read, her head bobbing. "How awful," she muttered.

She was there in the rear view, which was on the night setting so everything was darker and the lights of the cars floated under the surface. There she was, maybe in the back seat, but just the ghost of her. Could be a pew, now that I think of it. Her hair was wet and there might have been a leech on her collarbone, or maybe it was a shadow. She took off her rose gold shell necklace and I felt her warmth as she leaned forward and put it around my neck as I drove. Then she sat back and hummed until she found the same pitch as the tires on the road, and by the time I reached the turnoff for Johnston's place, she had become a copy of last week's Sundre Roundup.

When I got home they were getting ready for bed. Dad grunted as he headed for the bathroom to brush his teeth and chuckle over the blue toilet water. Mom was in the dark kitchen with the fridge door open and I knew she'd forgotten why she was there. She looked at me, her face stretched by the way cold bent the light from the fridge, the way the Johnston's slough warped to make the starport for Shell. I saw the retinal shimmer of the cataract in her left eye, the way she looked me as straight in the eyes as she could, then refocussed on the gold.

That's hers," Mom said. Snick.

Oil's up. Grain's up. Beer is what it is. Going to be the architect of my own need.

THE SMUT STORY

Disabling that economic structure in order to encourage self-discovery, intelligent relations, individual sexual freedom, and sexual transcendence on a routine basis would violate the sanctity of the marketplace, the shrine within which this cultural, sexual discourse occurs. The failure or disabling of individual imagination, so impoverishing to our sexual and emotional lives, enriches the pornographers.

And that, of course, is why we are not encouraged to be our own pornographers.

— from Candas Jane Dorsey's "Being One's Own
Pornographer" (as quoted by T.i.o. Boop)

III

Press Conference
March 14, 2010
Leva Cappucino Bar
Edmonton, AB

Let me be perfectly clear.

The Hermen collective does not know the current whereabouts of Mr. (or Ms.) T. Boop. Any one of us would happily testify under oath that he (or she) was without a doubt one of the most attractive women (or men) we have ever seen. However, try as we might — and trust me, we have tried — we cannot come up with a consistent description. Nor do any of Hermen's members have any knowledge of Ms. (or Mr.) Boop beyond the events of Hermen's Erotica and Pornography Night, now more commonly known as the Mother's Day Affair.

Certain local pundits have suggested that the mere scheduling of such an event on Mother's Day was in poor taste. The Hermen collective respectfully disagrees. Indeed, we would argue that any attempt, whether implicit or explicit, to repress (or deny) the obvious connections between motherhood and sex is at best misguided. Fuck the virgin-whore dichotomy. However, regardless of any abstract moral(istic) quibbles surrounding the underlying concept and timing of the event itself, the following statement is intended to address some of the more pointed allegations — particularly those of a certain Peter Smith — that have recently resurfaced in several print venues. To wit, Hermen can neither confirm nor deny reports of a "post-reading orgy" following the Mother's Day reading of May 10, 2009.

The collective would have preferred not to respond to these allegations at all, since if you weren't there it's none of your damn business. I mean, seriously. Why do you care? Seems to me you're probably getting off on this too. Nonetheless, given the frequency and persistence of these allegations, as well as the overwhelming public response to said allegations — both censorious and supportive — legal counsel has advised this statement as a necessary compromise.

First, Hermen would like to point out that the lack of credible, mutually corroborating first-hand witnesses to the events in question makes their very existence a matter of dispute. Certain publications have described these alleged events as "improper," "lewd," and even "obscene," and have further argued on this basis that Hermen should be investigated and prosecuted as a "common bawdy house." It is our position that such accusations are not only baseless but quite possibly libellous. And just for the record, Mr. Smith in particular should feel free to go fuck himself.

Nor does Hermen wish to comment on the recent birth of Eva, whose surname will not be repeated here, in deference to her mother's wishes — unlike certain writers working with thinly veiled "anonymous" sources, some of whom we could easily identify were we so inclined. However, unlike some people, we hold a healthy respect for the deep vulnerability and resultant expectation of privacy implicit in certain forms of intimate communication, even the privacy of those individuals who seem (apparently) constitutionally incapable of respecting our own. Nor will we speculate on the connections between Eva's birth and the alleged events of that night just over nine months ago. Nonetheless, we both can and do offer our congratulations to Eva's mother on the arrival of her healthy baby girl.

Furthermore, while the Hermen collective can neither confirm nor deny the post-reading events in question, we do affirm that to the best of our knowledge whatever may or may not have happened on the night of the reading was a matter of personal choice on the part of any and all alleged participants. Indeed, none of the published reports to the contrary (and yes, we have read them all) have included even a single first-hand account to corroborate their claims. On this point, even Mr. Smith's morally outraged, symptomatically vague, yet strangely persistent "anonymous" sources have remained uncharacteristically silent.

What Hermen can confirm are the basic events of the reading itself, which were as follows. At seven p.m., Hermen's Erotica and Pornography Night opened its doors to an audience of approximately five, a number which grew closer to twenty by the start of the reading. At eight o'clock, Joel Katelnikoff introduced the theme for the evening, noting that the order of performances would be changed due to the conspicuous absence of the first reader. (At this point, Mr. Katelnikoff may or may not have made certain comments about the absent reader's mother.) Stephanie Bailey then introduced the (formerly) second and third readers, whose pieces were performed without incident and generally well-received.

During the break, an audience member approached Mr. Katelnikoff and offered to fill in for the missing reader with a piece entitled "(The Importance Of) Being One's Own Pornographer." This audience member was, of course, the now-infamous T. Boop. In consultation with the rest of the collective, Mr. Katelnikoff agreed to include Boop's piece as a preferable alternative to cutting the reading short. Mark Woytiuk, in the course of this consultation, further commented that, "If nothing else, she's got a great voice." This statement prompted double-takes from certain group members but passed without further comment.

The performances resumed with the third reader, whose piece was also well-received, after which Ms. Bailey introduced "Mr." T. Boop — again prompting double-takes from several audience members — as a newcomer to Hermen. She also read Boop's supplied introduction, which consisted solely of an epigraph quoted from Candas Jane Dorsey's "Being One's Own Pornographer." Audience members have universally described Boop as a powerfully attractive person of indeterminate age, average height and build, and nondescript dress. Boop's gender, however, remains unknown, with various audience members recalling the reader as distinctly — and even notably — female, transgendered, androgynous, or male.

What? No, convenient is not at all the word I would use.

It's hardly convenient for us to have to try to explain any of this. Personally — and I'm sure that in this I speak for everyone who was there — I would much prefer to know who Boop really was. Not to mention, I for one would very much like to see (and especially hear) her again. Now please, if you could just let me finish.

All agree that the piece was structured as a nested second-person narrative, describing an unnamed "you" recounting an explicitly pornographic first-person anecdote to her (or his) unnamed lover.

Audience members further reported that their immediate surroundings seemed to "recede" or "fall away" under the influence of Boop's voice, a voice described alternatively as "sonorous," "soft-spoken," "deep," "childlike," "husky," or even "operatic." Myself, I would call it melodious, even musical. Or incantatory, like a spell...

But where was I? Ah yes.

In spite of broad agreement regarding the structure and subjective effect of the piece — succinctly described by Hermen organizer Eleni Loutas as "one for the spank bank" — no two members of the audience (or the Hermen collective, for that matter) recall T. Boop's story as depicting the same narrative. Depending on the individual, the story may be recalled as containing explicit scenes of homosexual, transvestite, transgendered, BDSM, incestuous, cross-generational, and even — in some instances — entirely vanilla, heterosexual sex. Thus, in spite of certain passages having been widely (and irresponsibly) reported as "verbatim" reproductions, the precise contents of Boop's reading, like the gender of the reader her- (or him-) self, remain unverifiable.

No, I don't expect you to believe anything. And frankly, I don't care. I'm sure you've all heard the expression you had to be there? Well in this case you really did. And you weren't. If you want to make up a story, feel free. But in that case, please recognize and acknowledge that that's what you're doing.

No, I'm not being facetious. Seriously, have fun with it. I know we have, and I expect we will continue to do so. But unlike some, we haven't printed every batshit crazy speculation that came into our heads as fact. And we would thank you to show the same restraint.

No, I...

That isn't what I said.

Look, do you want me to finish or not?

During Boop's performance, certain audience members saw fit to slam down their glasses, noisily gather their belongings, and pointedly exit the premises. (It should of course go without saying that none of these early-departing audience members have the slightest idea what may or may not have happened after the reading. So please bear that in mind when interviewing your "sources," anonymous or otherwise.) Nonetheless, in spite of these interruptions, the piece continued successfully to its conclusion, at which point Boop referred back to his (or her) bio/epigraph, explicitly encouraging audience members to become their own pornographers by expanding upon her (or his) story in conversation amongst themselves.

Seriously? No seriously, how the hell would I know that?

Look, if you want to know what Peter Smith and his so-called "sources" are on about, you're going to have to ask him yourself. We would have been happy to talk to him at any point in this process, but he hasn't contacted us. In fact, we have tried to contact him repeatedly over the past nine months, but he hasn't returned any of our calls. He hasn't talked to any of us since... Well, let's just say he hasn't consulted us on any of his articles.

Like I said, you'd have to ask him.

And while you're at it, maybe ask him what he was doing that night.

Now please. I'm almost done.

It is the official position of the Hermen collective that any conversations, storytelling, or other interactions which arose and/or continued at this point — whether on the premises or elsewhere — were entirely private and therefore remain beyond the ability (or right) of the Hermen collective to either report or comment upon. Nonetheless, the collective affirms and supports the right of Ms. (or Mr.) Boop to present his (or her) work in whatever form and venue she (or he) may choose. And we encourage him (or her) to continue to do so. Indeed, we would be honoured to have her (or him) perform with us again were he (or she) so inclined.

For although the alleged post-reading events can be neither confirmed nor denied, many of the alleged participants in these alleged activities have (allegedly) described said activities as quite enjoyable indeed. Hermen's official stance on the alleged events themselves, however, can be summarized in two words: "No comment."

II

For Eva S—
c/o L&P Associates
Barristers & Solicitors
Edmonton, AB
To be delivered on the occasion of her 18th birthday.[1]

10 May 2015,

Dearest Eva,

If all goes as we hope, this letter will be redundant by the time you receive it. But we have no way of guaranteeing that will be the case. So this is our insurance policy, a hedge against the unthinkable. Hopefully, its contents won't come as a complete surprise. No matter what others may have told you (especially Peter), please bear with us. You need to hear this.

For me, the memory always starts with that late spring, approaching-solstice light. The time warp kicks in the day all the clocks spring ahead, throwing everything subtly (but distinctly) off-kilter. The sun glows golden, hanging low on the horizon for hours, and the whole world becomes an instantly nostalgic, time-faded photograph of itself.

---

[1] Editor's Note: Eva S is believed to have celebrated her 18th birthday on February 14, 2028. However, although many scholars and biographers have accepted Eva's claim that her receipt of the long-delayed "Eighteen Year Letter" — as it has come to be known — was precisely what inspired her earliest work, the question of when (and indeed whether) she actually received and read the letter, as well as her direct or indirect reactions to its contents, remain ultmately unverifiable.

At first the effect is entirely subliminal. On a sunny afternoon, you might sit down at a cafe or patio or wherever. Doesn't matter what you're doing. Maybe you get absorbed, maybe not. Maybe you're bored as hell. But at a certain point, you look up from whatever you're doing (or not) and think, "Hey, I should eat something." Only to find the dinner hour passed, evening having long since given way to full night without the slightest hint of a transition. The light has fooled your body and mind, both retroactively awakening to the hunger that has haunted you for quite some time, only now springing full-blown into consciousness.

Every year, the slow-changing light draws me back into that same odd surrealism, a disjunction arising from a conflict between subconscious expectations and the material reality of living in this particular part of the world, at this particular time of year.

Always, it takes me like a dream.

It's May 2009 as I walk slowly, almost reluctantly, towards the reading. Mother's Day has drained these residential streets of activity, a vaguely post-apocalyptic desertion: abandoned toys on lawns, yard and gardening tools set aside, all the signs of a sudden departure. Elsewhere, restaurants are packed, parking near impossible, reservations the ultimate currency of the day. But here, Mom's night off prefigures the end of the world.

Leva materializes on the corner, a former convenience store converted to a retro Italian organic café. Broad windows across the north and west sides admit the late-afternoon light, transforming the round marble tabletops and chrome-and-plastic stools into something out of a foreign film. In the back, windowless portion of the room, a row of black-and-chrome espresso machines gleams darkly. Behind the counter, organic food, fancy coffees, and a strategically limited selection of exotic alcohols are available to those who can recognize and properly name them. Both the staff and clientele are much younger and hipper than I ever was.

As I look around, my dubious distinction as the oldest guy in the room slowly sinks in. My beige T-shirt, green hoodie, black chucks, and blue jeans suddenly feel more try-hard than inconspicuous. I had hoped to blend into the crowd, but only eight people have arrived so far. Nine including me. Recognizing no one, I take a table by myself, wishing I had brought along a book or a notebook or something to make me look occupied. Instead, I pretend to stare out the window, watching the half-transparent images of surrounding hipster kids reflected in the glass. Like a child hiding under covers, I'm convinced that if I don't look directly at the Monster then it won't see me, and I'll be okay. Effectively invisible.

Or perhaps I'm both monster and child. Monster in the sense of the creepy older guy, slimy old porn-junkie emerging from his basement in search of like-minded company. Child in the sense of naïveté and disorientation. Why am I even here? Sure, I've seen porn. Who hasn't? But I don't really get it. Perhaps my casual googling was insufficient, a proper pornographic education requiring more dedication to the form. Whatever. Everything I found was boring, too mechanistic, disconnected, misogynist, or just plain weird. Seriously. Who gets off on this stuff? But perhaps I'm missing the point. Or perhaps that is the point. To see if there's something else out there. Or rather, out here. Something between the bullshit happily-ever-after fairy tale of a romance novel (not that I've ever read one) and the empty hump and grind of internet porn. Something actually sexy. I don't know.

All I know is that I have never felt quite so straight as I do at this moment. Not straight as in heterosexual, but straight as in square. Tete carré, as the Quebecois might put it. A hapless voyeur in the land of the young. My first exposure to the very idea of sex came from playground jokes, kids who knew little more than I did, which was next to nothing. Dirty jokes whose dirtiness arose almost entirely from their incomprehensibility, the knowing chuckle we all quickly learned to fake. But these hipster-kids have grown up (insofar as they have) swimming in a virtual sea of porn. It's an everyday fact of living in a world where the internet, for as long as they can remember and beyond, has always existed. In such a context, even the most explicit displays of bodily extrusions and orifices, arranged in any imaginable configuration, must carry little more impact than one of those tasteless playground jokes. Or so I imagine.

I stare out the window, half-watching the slow arrivals trickle in, more hipster kids, some guy in a suit who looks almost as out of place as me. Dissociate into that all-encompassing light. Let it subsume my discomfort into the deeper surrealism of the season. Absorb.

I have no recollection of her entry.

One moment, I'm drifting awash in light, and the next she is simply there. A shadow coalescing in shades of black: T-shirt, jeans, chucks, and a hoodie. Like me, minus the awkward self-consciousness and chromatic variety. I follow her reflection in the window. Dark hair in a pageboy bob frames narrow features, her body thin to the point of boyishness yet somehow obviously, even aggressively, feminine. Can't pin down an age, so I'm assuming way too young. I risk my first direct glance of the evening to find her smiling. At me. Dark eyes and a quirked eyebrow. I revert back to my window-gazing, and by the time I look again she's taken a seat directly between me and the microphone. Alone. The crowd quiets as the reading begins.

The first reader passes in a blur. He probably thinks I'm entranced — and I am, but not by him. I can't take my eyes off Hoodie Woman. I watch her reaction to the reading, which has something to do with animal sex and the circle of life. Deleuze meets The Lion King meets Nietzsche or some such nonsense. She looks... nonplussed, and I can practically hear her thoughts. Porn and erotica? This?

I agree. Deleuze? I mean, I get the sapiophile thing, but that's still one hell of a stretch. He could have at least gone with Irigaray or Cixous. Thankfully, the reader finishes quickly and scurries back to his seat, his departure accompanied by polite applause.

Next up, an older woman reads a piece about porn-watching teen-aged boys, a note-perfect depiction of their reactions to hardcore porn in the semi-public social setting of a basement rec-room. Her wry description of the wah-wah guitars, bad dialogue, and orifice-filling frenzy of bad porn makes me chuckle, and her recounting of the boys' crass overcompensation for their own sexual inexperience — manifesting in a series of increasingly tasteless and even downright offensive 14-year-old-boy commentary — makes me cringe in recognition. Yet even through the most explicit scenes, she keeps her eyes fixed on the text before her, no shift in expression beyond the occasional introspective smile. As if she's simply watching these events unfold on a small eight-and-a-half-by-eleven screen and reporting them back to us in real time. Beneath the satire, I hear an undercurrent of sympathy for the boys' naïveté, and I wonder if she has teenaged boys of her own. If so, I doubt they realize how lucky they are.

Hoodie Woman tilts her head back and closes her eyes, exposing the delicate curve of her throat. Lips part, breath visibly deepening as her hands open wide. Fingers grasping at air as the piece winds to its end, a final image of the boys' inevitably impending wet dreams. On the final line, her hands clench and eyes snap open, locking onto the reader. A silent, full-body shiver, then another, and her fists release. The reader looks up for the first time and freezes, snared by Hoodie Woman's eyes, that focused stare. The reader's eyes widen, and I have to look away.

When I look back, the reader has turned bright red, her gaze pinned to the floor before her. She murmurs a closing thank you, and the applause is immediate and enthusiastic as she walks swiftly back to her seat, still avoiding all eye contact. The emcee encourages us to refresh our drinks for the next set and immediately follows her own advice, beelining to the counter for a glass of white wine. She downs it, orders another, then sips the second while casting occasional, darting glances over at Hoodie Woman. So it's not just me.

As the slow wave of between-sets conversation rises, anticipation crackles through the room like an approaching prairie storm. Everyone talks at once, trying (and failing) to defuse that unspoken, building tension. Hoodie Woman sits alone at the eye of the storm, surveying the room and its inhabitants, sipping her red wine in silence. I also sit in silence, racking my brain for some way to start a conversation. I have to meet her. As I half-rise to walk over and give it a shot, a voice emerges from the surrounding hum.

"Is this seat taken?" A thin blonde woman stands next to me, her hand on the back of the unoccupied chair where I've set my jacket. She looks nervous. "I mean, if you're saving it... "

"No. No, not at all." I smile (reassuringly, I hope), transfer my jacket from the empty chair to the back of my own, and again begin to stand. "In fact, if you could save my seat... " But now Hoodie Woman is deep in conversation with one of the organizers. Too slow.

I sit back down.

"Thanks!" says the blonde. "I mean, if you're sure that's okay."

"No really, I'd love the company." Still, she hesitates. "I was actually feeling a bit conspicuous. You know, guy sitting alone at a porn reading." Sure, that'll make her feel real comfortable. "I uh... I mean, really, it's no problem. All yours." I push the chair in her direction.

She sits but seems paralyzed by the question of where to put her jacket and purse. The stutter-step rhythm of her movements reminds me of a squirrel. She tries the table first, then pauses. A quick half-move towards her lap, another longer pause, and a decisive flurry of action, purse under chair, coat draped over the back. "I mean, I got here late," she resumes, settled now but speech still echoing that same stuttering rhythm. "And I stood at the bar for the first set, but." A half-second pause, then all in one breath, "But then I noticed this seat but I wasn't sure if it was free or not so I just waited for the break and now... Well... Hi."

We shake hands. More organizers surround Hoodie Woman. And though they outnumber her four to one, they're the ones who look nervous.

"So have you been to a lot of these things?" The blonde's question pulls me back. "I mean, is this how they usually go?" She's cute, I realize, but not intimidatingly so. A hint of hot-librarian with muted vegan undertones. Her glasses are big, round, clunky things, and she wears no makeup. Like her clothes, the glasses are too plain and lacking in irony to be fashionable with this crowd. Not vintage, just aging and a bit out of date. Like me.

"Actually, I have no idea," I admit. "It's my first time too. It's... interesting."

"That's one word for it." She smiles, calmer now, and catches me glancing at Hoodie Woman, who is laughing with the last reader, the woman who couldn't meet her eye just a few minutes ago. The blonde chin-nods. "Friend of yours?"

I blush. "No, we've never... I mean, I guess I just... "

"Oh, I know exactly what you mean." She chuckles, openly staring at the object of my not-as-covert-as-I-thought attention. "You know, for the life of me I couldn't tell you what the first two readers looked like?"

The emcee's introduction of the next set cuts off my response.

A woman in the audience hands off the newborn in her lap to the man beside her, stands, and approaches the microphone. She has that T-shirt-and-overalls look of a new mom, totally at ease in her own physicality, and she launches directly into a piece exploring pre-, during-, and post-pregnancy sex in explicit and erotic detail. The blonde blushes right up to her hairline, and for the first time tonight I feel like the voyeur I earlier imagined myself to be. This reader makes unflinching eye-contact with individual audience members, some for just a few words, others for a full line or more. She saves Hoodie Woman for last, finally meeting her gaze and holding it through an entire stanza, mingling images of breastfeeding, labour, and orgasm to close on a sustained climax of milk and blood and cum.

No one makes a sound.

A single clap. Then another. Hoodie Woman applauds alone, still holding that gaze. Then she smiles and nods, a brief head-dip of respect freeing the reader to deliver two ringing thank yous, one to Hoodie Woman, the second to the room at large. The answering applause is thunderous, including a few hoots and whistles. The reader returns to her seat, retrieves her child, and nods back to Hoodie Woman over the nestling newborn's head. Then she calmly unhooks an overall strap, lifts her shirt, and latches the child to her breast to nurse.

Still applauding, the emcee returns to the microphone and introduces the final reader as "Mr. T. Boop." I think I am ready for anything. Until Hoodie Woman pushes back her chair, stands, and slowly walks to the front. She takes her time, lightly touching the emcee's arm and leaning forward to whisper something in her ear before turning to face us.

No, not us. Me. Her eyes lock on mine. A wave of vertigo.

Then the adrenaline jolt. Accelerated heart rate, breath turning shallow and fast, a deep hop in the gut as that swooping moment of freefall stretches. A powerful desire to hide, and a strong thread of fear. Fear and panic and paralysis (still pinned by those eyes), and at first the only thought I can muster is oh fuck. Then: Holy shit, I really want this person.

And it scares the shit out of me.

Her eyes expand, pupils dilating impossibly large as the room fades and recedes. Darkness creeps in at the edge of my vision, the chair beneath me and the table I lean on turning abstract, fluid, and nebulous. And though I know I must still be sitting in the chair, still gripping the table, my feet and hands float in empty space as gravity contorts, convulses, and vanishes. Her face a final beacon in the surrounding darkness. Then that disappears too.

I shake my head. Blink furiously. No change. Just the strangely muted sound of my own breathing. It doesn't echo or reverberate. It is absorbed. As if the darkness were a sponge, soaking up every light, sound, touch, and smell to leave me floating alone in perfect isolation. Except for her. I can't see her, but I know she's here.

The darkness is warm and humid. If it weren't for the slightest warm breath against my corneas, I wouldn't know if my eyes were open or closed.

Close them for several seconds. Deliberately turn my head. Open.

The room shimmers like heat-wave haze over summer blacktop then slowly swims into focus. The espresso machines in the back, the Euro-minimalist décor, the setting sun a bit lower, but still there. The light, the world, and all the objects within it have returned. But the silence remains. No background chatter. No clinking of dishes, cutlery, or glasses, no whispered orders at the front counter. No soft rustle of people shifting in their seats.

I scan the audience to either side, carefully avoiding even the slightest glance towards the front of the room. Some stare blankly in the same direction I avoid. Are they trapped in the space I just escaped? Others, like me, blink and shake their heads, averting their eyes as I do. The latter shy away from direct eye contact, as if that singular gaze might be contagious, each pair of eyes a trap waiting to be sprung. A flurry of noise and motion at the far end of the room as first one man, then a woman, then others, slam down their glasses and mugs, hastily gather their belongings, and head for the door. A few more hurried exits, the door slamming once, twice, three times. The full exodus takes no more than a minute or two. A final slam of the door, and silence returns. The only sound, that of the crowd's soft, slow respiration. Only a few remain who have thus far avoided (or escaped) the gravity well of Tia's eyes. Any who glance in her direction, however briefly, are instantly caught.

Finally, she speaks. A whisper so soft it should be hard to hear. But it's not.

"This story is not for reading, but for telling. Not for you, but for your lover. This is the story of a story of a story... "

I listen to Tia's story, which is also my story. It is beyond porn. No distanced, controlling camera. No distance at all. Not apart from me, but a part of me. A reflective, amplifying feedback loop. Her voice lifts me up and pulls me in, a wave of sound evading all internal censors to draw out my most intimate sensual fantasies, my most secret desires. Drawing them out only to return them to me, shared and multiplied in the amplifying echo of a lover's growing arousal. In response to this story. My story. A story of lips and skin and tongue. Of taste and touch. Slowly, with a growing (yet achingly restrained) urgency, the story builds.

A ragged gasp at my side pulls me back.

The blonde surfaces as I did, shaking her head and breathing heavily. Her shoulders hunch, white-knuckled hands gripping the marble tabletop. A pause, then she pushes herself up to look around the room. Our eyes meet, and we mirror each other's confusion across the small table as Tia's story continues. Progressively colonizing our senses, it expands. I can still see the blonde breathing — almost hyperventilating now — but the sound is gone. She looks down at her feet, squares her shoulders, and takes a long, slow breath. When she looks back up, she smiles and shrugs as if to say, Hey, if you can't beat 'em... Then she takes one more deep breath like a swimmer about to dive, and turns to face Tia.

And though my resistance is waning, breath grown ragged and muscles tensing under the story's growing influence, I can still focus just enough to see the full process. The electric jolt of initial contact, her entire body stiffening. A soft gasp (seen not heard), eyes widening, pupils instantly dilated. Then the tension passes, shoulders release, and her lips part slightly, curving upwards as she willingly surrenders to her own world-engulfing arousal.

In that moment, she is absolutely fucking gorgeous.

Time and space vanish. Only the story remains.

The room slowly coalesces in half-silvered café windows, and as Tia concludes with thanks and an exhortation for us to share our own stories, I watch its reflection, returning. I have forgotten nothing, details as fresh and vivid now as they will remain for years to come. But the compulsion to watch Tia has vanished. Now, I want to see everyone else.

A few formerly occupied tables sit entirely empty. Those who remain stare as openly as I do. And suddenly everyone — every single person — is inexpressibly beautiful. I meet several pairs of eyes and never once feel the urge to look away. Around the room, glances meet, and these universally flushed cheeks clearly have nothing to do with embarrassment. My eyes wander back across the room to settle on the blonde beside me. Like every other person, she sits entirely unchanged. Like every other person, she is transformed. Our eyes meet and hold. Then she smiles, and I smile back. And we begin to talk.

First, we talk about the story. She shares her version, I mine. They start off the same but rapidly diverge into completely different (though equally explicit) narratives. And when first a man, then two more women and another man join us, the sharing expands to incorporate each new arrival's story, divergences multiplying and growing ever wilder. Given the content, the conversation is strangely effortless. At first we avoid touching, but incidental contacts accumulate, prompting shared smiles, more expansive gestures. Hands brushing across the table, a chance jostling of shoulders, a hand on a shoulder or the back of a neck.

When the subject of Tia herself comes up — and here there is some debate as to whether it was *Tia* or *Tio* — we discover that she, like her story, manifested differently for each person. Depending on the viewer, she was male, female, trans, androgynous, fat, thin, both light and dark haired, light and dark skinned. One woman insists she was wearing a mask. No one seems particularly concerned by these discrepancies. We're more interested in the stories.

Only much later does it occur to one of the women to wonder if Tio (or Tia) might want to join our conversation. But when we finally look around and try to locate her (or him), we find that he (or she) is gone.

Not much more to tell, really. Where the audience had arrived in quiet singles, pairs, and trios, it left in talkative quads, quints, and sextuples. Our group adjourned to Jamie's place — yes, *that* Jamie[2] — where we continued sharing stories. No longer merely recounting, we started embellishing with increasingly collaborative interjections. I think it was Peter who started that, though some of the others remember it differently. By that time, everyone was talking at once so it's hard to say for sure. Some additions were funny, others downright strange. Later, none of us could pinpoint exactly when we shifted from telling to showing.

When the six of us awoke the next morning, there was no sense of awkwardness as we dressed, exchanged phone numbers, and agreed to keep in touch. And incredibly, we did. Except for Peter. Within a week he stopped returning our calls, and the number he gave us was disconnected a few weeks later. That was disappointing, but aside from your mother no one was particularly worried. Right from the start, Peter seemed more solid than anyone, generally grounded, stable, and competent in the world. Shows how much we knew.

Later, as your mother's pregnancy became more apparent — and yes, of course she was "the blonde" — it seemed only natural for her and Jamie to rent a house, and the rest of us moved in one at a time as our respective leases ran out. And then there was you.

---

[2] Editor's Note: Although Jamie's identity has never been confirmed, it seems reasonable to assume that this is the same person Eva S often refers to in her own writings as "Uncle" — or occasionally "Auntie" — Jamie, who is generally assumed to be one of her five co-parents. If one believes Eva S's version of her own history.

How to explain these last five years? The incredible moment of your arrival, the brief but intense battle we fought to have all five of us present in the delivery room when the home-birth turned complicated and we ended up in a hospital after all? Those first few months? You have changed us all, and (almost) all for the better. We foresaw none of this, but we wouldn't change a thing. Well, except for Peter. As you no doubt know by now, he didn't take it well.

The rest, I'm sure, is fairly obvious. Or should be if things have gone as we hope. But Peter's raising a stink again. At first it was just letters to the editor, a few op-eds, all that crap about the reading. We tried to contact him, left messages inviting him to come visit any time, that we considered him as much your parent as any of us. But he got it in his head that people "like us" (whatever that means) aren't fit to raise a child. After he got married, he upped his game, turned the whole thing into a legal battle, starting with (failed) demands for paternity testing (which would have required your mother's consent), then suing for custody on broader "moral" grounds. For a while none of it went anywhere, but now he's got some serious backing. Some conservative "family values" group, which we're thinking must mean he hasn't told them everything. And that's good, might give us some leverage if push comes to shove. Still, even if they ditch Peter along the way, these family value thugs might still go after us in court, try to set a legal precedent or something. Thus this insurance policy.

We *hope* that none of this is necessary, that we're being overly paranoid and worrying for nothing. But the fact is, if you're receiving this letter, we have no way of knowing what you may think of us by now. A lot can happen in thirteen years. And we wanted to make sure you at least knew your own history. You deserve at least that much. So if we haven't been able to tell you this story ourselves, we hope you will at least consider the possibility that there is *absolutely nothing wrong or shameful about you and where you came from*. Whatever second thoughts Peter may have had, and whatever he may have told you, you were conceived and raised — insofar and for as long as we were able — in a space of joy and love and celebration.

We also figured this was probably the closest you could get to meeting Tia (or Tio). And since she (or he) is in some ways as much your parent as any one of the six of us — and yes, that includes Peter — we thought you at least deserved to know. First, where you came from, and how, and under what circumstances. Second, that we believe in you. Even now, I can hear you laughing in the next room. And for this I will always be grateful. May you always hold onto that incredible joy. And may you never have to receive this letter.

I

A Note on the (Missing) Text(s)[3]

This story is not for reading, but for telling. Not for you, but for your lover.

This is the story of a story of a story. If it happens to turn you on, that is nothing more than a side effect. Like sex, it can take a thousand different forms, but it always progresses through a narrative: beginning, middle, end (. . . and end... and end...). As much as you might wish it — and you often do — no single instance can go on forever. This story is collaborative. You tell it with as well as to your lover. And always, the story starts not with your lover, but with you.

It is, after all, your story.

Thus begins — and ends — the only verifiable surviving fragment of "(The Importance Of) Being One's Own Pornographer," as performed

---

[3] Excerpted from Dr. Maria Quinlan's introduction to the 2059 edition of *The Smut Story: Critical Reflections* (Vanitate Books), released in honour of the (alleged) fiftieth anniversary of the Mother's Day Affair.

by the mysterious Tio Boop.[4] Whether or not one believes that this performance ever happened, its seminal (or perhaps ovarian) influence on Eva S's work remains undeniable.[5] Boop's inexhaustible (and by all accounts unforgettable) story haunts the study of Eva S's work at every turn, echoing down the decades to reverberate in every scholarly paper, every ethnographic study of Eva S fandom, and every Eva S performance. Even so, in producing the first edition of this volume, my co-editors and I agreed that it would be best to omit any transcriptions of Tio Boop's original story, acknowledging its central importance only through the title.[6] And although I have expanded this edition with several more recent critical reconsiderations of Eva S's oeuvre, I still stand by that decision.

Certainly, numerous "transcriptions" of Boop's story are available from both online and print sources, and though the contents vary wildly, each one opens with the passage quoted above and echoes the

---

[4] This passage is technically "verifiable" only in the sense that it is the sole fragment of Tio Boop's story to remain consistent across all versions and to have been both endorsed and circulated by Eva S. However, the original source of this fragment remains a matter of significant scholarly dispute.

[5] While many believe that Eva S has empirically verified the contents of the Boop passage cited above through her ongoing collection of first-hand accounts from the original reading, others argue that she may have invented the "collection" itself (at least initially) in an attempt to imagine what attendees might have heard and what such accounts might have sounded like, had any existed. Still others contend that the Eighteen Year Letter, Tio Boop, and even the Mother's Day Affair itself are nothing more than an elaborate hoax (or performance piece) designed to mythologize Eva S's critical engagement with her own artistic practice and philosophy. However, neither I nor my former co-editors subscribe to any of these overly elaborate theories, preferring instead to take Ms. S at her word.

[6] Although they have declined to append their names to this edition, I must thank Doctors Linda Martin and John Torres, co-editors of the original 2044 edition of *The Smut Story,* for their contributions to the text. I still believe that our differing perspectives — and occasionally vigorous debates — ultimately made this volume the success it has been for the past fifteen years. Nonetheless, we all agreed then, as I believe now, that referencing "The Smut Story" — the colloquial term by which Smutsters the world over now refer to Tio Boop's original story — in the title constituted the perfect acknowledgement of Ms. (or Mr.) Boop's contribution both to Eva's work and to this volume.

underlying structure described in Hermen's 2010 press conference.[7] However, the most reliable versions of Boop's story remain accessible only through Eva S's extensive audio archive of first-hand oral accounts of the original reading.[8] As the self-appointed guardian and archivist of the Smut Story — which she often cites as the primary inspiration for her own career as an erotic performance artist[9] — Ms. S strictly regulates access to these recordings, keeping them available

---

[7] Like the original reading, the events of the Hermen press conference cannot be verified via the public record, although all of the organizers named in the (alleged) press conference transcript agree that it is accurate insofar as they can recall. Indeed, to date, the only "verified" attendees to either the original Mother's Day Affair or the subsequent press conference are the Hermen organizers themselves, since even second-hand published accounts — such as those the aforementioned transcript attributes to "Peter Smith" — have been lost, presumably erased by the info-liberationist (or, according to some, info-terrorist) group known only as "We."

[8] Eva S has been collecting these stories for decades, having issued a call in 2030 (which remains open) for anyone who remembers Tio Boop's original performance to visit the archive in person and recite his (or her) story in its entirety. These recitations are recorded directly to audio files, thus preserving the precise nuance, intonation, and rhythm of each storyteller's voice, which Eva S maintains is an utterly crucial aspect of the project.

[9] Eva S's iconic breakout performance piece, "Fuck(ing) the Pope" (2029), has remained available online since its original (unauthorized) filming, the posting of which prompted an immediate firestorm of debate that has been well-documented elsewhere. (For insightful discussion of the shifting social and moral anxieties attached to these debates by various groups in the fifteen years following the video's release, see Sharon Riddle's "'Blasphemy,' 'Obscenity,' 'Pornography,' and 'Art' as (Sub)Cultural Diagnostics: Mapping 'Moral' Readings of Eva S's 'Fuck(ing) the Pope' from 2029 to 2044.") To date, Eva has declined to comment on whether the sex and orgasms were real or simulated, or whether the recorded audience reactions were spontaneous or a scripted part of the performance. The priest in this video has long since been identified (and defrocked) and has likewise declined to comment on the real or simulated nature of his own participation. Eva's career since then — from the early live performances to her later audio sculptures, which range from the conceptual ("Fidelity," 2047) to the ironically pornographic ("Seventies Bush," 2048) — has likewise been well-documented in both popular media and a variety of scholarly publications. For further reading on Eva S's artistic trajectory from internet porn sensation to subcultural icon to internationally respected performance artist, see Jonathan Torres' landmark critical monograph, *Pornography and/as Art: The Rise of a Reluctant Icon* (2049).

to the public on two conditions: (1) that no recording devices may be used to reproduce or transmit these stories beyond the archive,[10] and (2) that no one may listen to these recordings in solitude but must be accompanied by at least one companion with whom they will discuss the story afterwards.[11] Once these conditions have been agreed to, visitors are free to browse the archive and listen as they choose.

After visitors have explored the archive, however, Eva S encourages them to share these stories in the spirit of the original reading, preferably in as open and public a venue as possible. (Indeed, the so-called Smutsters have enthusiastically adopted this directive in both their guerrilla performances and more formal readings, which range from the impromptu and improvised to more "authentic" repro-

---

[10] Accessed by a gravel laneway, Eva S's estate consists of an aging two-storey farmhouse on a half-acre lot with a spacious garden, several fruit-bearing trees, and a broad, well-kept lawn. No fences or other obvious external security systems distinguish the home from any others in the area, and the archive is housed in a modest addition out back. However, while the estate is open to physical visitors, it is a technological fortress. All virtual intrusions — from neural interfaces to nanotechnology shunts to neutrino-enabled networking prostheses — are strictly regulated by some of the most sophisticated security systems in existence. All wireless communications are blocked from the estate boundary onward, and either Eva or one of her assistants meets all visitors at the door, producing a detailed list of forbidden technology which must be surrendered before entering the house. (Although no scanners are in evidence, the list is invariably comprehensive, detailed, and specific to each visitor.) One presumes that these security systems have been supplied by We, for whom cyber-privacy has always been a central concern, and of whom Eva S has long been a strong and vocal supporter. Indeed, various governments have attempted to requisition the estate's scanning technology in the name of national security, but all such demands have subsequently been quietly withdrawn, likely under direct pressure from We.

[11] In the case of visitors arriving alone, Eva S or one of her assistants will typically take on this companion role. Indeed, in my own solo visits, Eva and her assistants have not only joined me for as many hours as I have chosen to listen but have also proven incredibly forthcoming in our subsequent explorations. Contrary to what one might expect from her aggressive stances and flamboyant accessorizing as a performer, Eva tends more towards comfort than style in dress. An older woman with greying hair, she often sips herbal tea as she calmly describes her own erotic reaction (or lack thereof) to the recording under discussion, occasionally slipping into reminiscences of the visitor who originally recited it. For anyone seeking to explore these stories, I would highly recommend such a visit.

ductions of the original Mother's Day event.)[12] Ms. S describes the maintenance (and oral dissemination) of this archive as her tribute to Tio Boop, without whose original reading she would quite literally not exist.[13] She further claims that through sharing these stories — and the

---

[12] The designation *Smutster* was originally coined in 2030 as a derogatory term for Eva S's exponentially growing legion of fans. However, the term was reappropriated almost immediately by those same fans and aggressively refined over the decades, such that it now refers more narrowly to aficionados of the Tio Boop stories rather than fans of Eva's work as a whole. The Smusters' "authentic" readings — although their authenticity has never been endorsed by Eva S as such — strive to reproduce the original Erotica and Pornography Night described in the Eighteen Year Letter as faithfully as possible. Traditionally, these events are held at a faux-European café (even in continental Europe, some faux-European cafés have sprung up to cater to purist Smutsters), with a row of espresso machines in the back, lighting systems rigged with slow-timed dimmers to mimic the fading Edmonton light, and as many additional supporting details as the organizers can manage. Each event opens with the alleged epigraph to Tio Boop's original reading and consists of four reading slots, including a last-minute reshuffle of the reading order due to the (also traditional) absence of the first reader. The final reading slot is typically held open in case Tio him or herself should show up, and when Tio invariably fails to arrive, the remainder of the reading may proceed in any number of ways. The final reader may be arranged in advance or selected from the audience, either by random ballot or some more spontaneous method, such as a blindfolded organizer picking a person from the crowd by touch alone. Some purists omit the final reading entirely, observing a minute of silence, while others read from bootleg transcripts of "original" stories allegedly heard at the 2009 event. Indeed, debates over the appropriate means of handling these finer details have often led to significant splits within the Smutster community. When participating in these events both as a fan in my teens and later while researching my master's thesis, I always preferred the minute of silence, during which — if only for a moment — I could close my eyes and imagine Tio right there in front of us, about to begin. However, even the most "authentic" of these readings stop short of reproducing — at least on any formal level — the post-reading events described in the Eighteen Year Letter. For an in-depth study of these practices within the broader context of the Smutster movement, see *Smutsters Unite! Sexual Revolution in the 21st Century: A Case Study* (Quinlan, 2045).

[13] Due to her status as one of the earliest and most thoroughly documented "We-orphans" of the late '20s and early '30s, no official records exist for Eva S before 2028. She maintains that she was raised by her five parents until the age of eight, when one of Peter Smith's legal challenges gained enough traction to have her removed from the family. However, Smith's concurrent bid for sole custody was unsuccessful, and Eva was placed into foster care until age eighteen, when she received two letters. The first, written as an "insurance policy" in case the worst happened and Peter succeeded in breaking up the family, described the unusual

intensive subjective engagement arising from this in-person sharing —
Tio Boop's purpose will inevitably manifest itself, that purpose being
not merely to titillate but to free people to share and explore their own
erotic fantasies and stories and, more importantly, to learn to enjoy
these stories without guilt or fear of reprisal.[14]

---

circumstances of Eva's conception. The second letter arrived enclosed with the
first, a cryptic missive from the group We, detailing Smith's ongoing harassment
of Eva's birth family even after her removal. In response, the family had accepted
an offer from We to erase all records of their existence, and now the organization
was making that same offer to Eva. Eva immediately accepted, thereby neutraliz-
ing Smith's harassment, and asked to be reunited with her family. Shortly after
this reunion, Eva began producing her own erotic performance art. Unlike many
early We-orphans, Eva was never brought up on charges of fraud or identity theft
(possibly because of her sudden fame) and was in fact a key promoter of We's
emergence into the public sphere in the late '20s. (Although it remains difficult to
determine with any certainty, anecdotal evidence suggests that We had been op-
erating covertly since at least 2004, and many We-orphans resorted to identity
theft as a means of survival.) However, it was not until We's cyber-erasure of
several world leaders in 2034 — including the acting President of the United
States — that worldwide legislative reform provided legal status to the growing
legion of We-orphans. To this day, despite her extraordinary candour regarding
the details of her own life, Eva has refused to identify anyone from her pre-We
past by either their current or "real" name. Certain scholars have argued that
Eva's entire backstory may be fabricated, but the demonstrable existence of
We — along with Eva's longstanding and well-documented connections to that
group — seems to support Eva's version of events. Moreover, I can personally
attest to at least some of We's activities around that time, since in 2028, when I
was thirteen, the group abruptly and thoroughly erased both my own and my father's files. To the best of my knowledge, this was the only time We ever erased
private citizens' files without their explicit request and permission.

[14] Over years of visiting the archive, first while researching my dissertation and
later in support of my ongoing scholarly work, I have found it impossible to pre-
dict how any given listener will react to a particular story. Furthermore, I can
personally attest to the fact that not all — indeed, not even the majority — of the
archived stories are titillating in the sense of provoking sexual excitement. Certainly, some do (and powerfully so), but others may be heard from a more
distanced, almost anthropological perspective. But however devoid of erotic impact (or even downright repulsive) they may be, a current of vulnerability runs
through them, a sense that each story somehow reflects the recorded speaker's
entirely uncensored erotic self. And with each new story, the listener may be
pulled further into the profoundly *human* character of each telling. Rather than
blurring together into a mind-numbing catalogue of increasingly banal and
mechanized sexual acts, each story becomes *more* particular, more visceral, more
differentiated from every one that came before. Indeed, over the course of several
stories, the listener may gain a stronger and stronger sense of having almost been

In her own work, in accord with her manifesto, Eva S has consistently aimed at enlarging the realm of erotic possibility, encouraging her audience (and the world at large) to move beyond the guilt so deeply and commonly ingrained in certain ways of looking at sex and sexual desire.[15] Her most recent work ("Long Time Coming," 2049), for example, explores the possibility that even the infamous "Peter Smith" may have been as much a victim as a proponent of the conservative "family values" he so vehemently espoused.[16] In it, noting the one in three chance that Mr. Smith was indeed her biological father, she explores how Smith's persistent guilt over his participation on the night of her conception could have fuelled his two-decade quest to reclaim the child he genuinely believed to be his daughter.[17] If, she

---

there for the original reading, as if slowly being convinced, cajoled, and freed to tell her own story in response, and this anachronistic sense of presence may help to explain how this archive of "original" stories has proliferated and expanded beyond all mathematical possibility to contain hundreds (possibly thousands) of stories. And yet, impossible or not, I have studied these stories and their variations for several decades now, and I can attest with great confidence — my former co-editors' objections notwithstanding — that *they are all genuine.*

[15] See Eva S's uncharacteristically direct "Manifesto" (2033), another early performance piece. See also Dulles and Candle's essay in Part 4 of this volume for an intriguing use of this piece as an interpretive lens through which to (re)read some of Eva's earliest work ("Manifesting the Manifesto: Exposures, Recoveries, and Complications of the 'Political' in Eva S's Early Performances").

[16] At various times, Peter claimed to be Eva's rightful guardian, her estranged uncle, and even her biological father, but since his attempts to force a DNA test failed, these claims remain unverified. In all his legal battles with Eva's family, Smith consistently appealed to "family values," thereby securing financial and legal support from a variety of conservative political and religious groups. Nonetheless, when one of these well-funded custody challenges proved (temporarily) successful in removing Eva from her family, Peter was disqualified as a suitable guardian on the basis of his own participation — however disavowed and regretted after the fact — in the "sordid" circumstances of her conception.

[17] My father and I were never close. He never approved of my studies and wasn't shy about saying so at every opportunity. Ever since I attended my first Smut Story reading at the age of fifteen, he hated what he called "that goddamn smut stuff" and found it intolerable that any daughter of his would demean herself by becoming involved with it in any way. Six months ago, for the first time, he told me why. He was, he said, the very same "Peter Smith" who had worked so hard to remove Eva from her family, and he sincerely believed he was her father. His

implies, Peter Smith had been free to construct his erotic self on his own terms — and to partake in the incredible erotic diversity of the world around him — he might not have felt such a compulsion to impose received notions of sexual morality upon his own former sexual partners.

Ultimately, this is why I have upheld the original decision to omit all transcriptions of Tio Boop's original story from this collection. Not, as my former co-editors insisted, because of their unreliability or potential to offend, but out of respect for the story itself. As Ms. (or Mr.) Boop so succinctly put it, this ever-proliferating story is not for reading, but for telling, and to pin it down to any singular or static representation would violate the very deepest principles of Boop's (and by extension Eva's) artistic project. Rather, I strongly encourage readers to visit the archive and hear these stories for themselves. Immerse yourself in them, surrender to their rhythms, their internal logic, and explore what sensations may come. Let them under your skin, where they can expose the contours of your own hidden stories. Then pass them on to friends, lovers, or even strangers — none of these being mutually exclusive categories, of course — along with your own, ultimately mingled and mixed, indistinguishable, the one from the other.[18]

---

voice shook as he apologized for disparaging my studies and told me how deeply he now regretted his nineteen-year persecution of Eva and her family. Then he entrusted me with what he called his own "Forty-nine Year Letter," which he asked me to deliver to Eva, sealed and in person, upon the event of his death. He also had me hold the microphone to his lips as he finally told the story he heard on that fateful night. This, I was to deliver into the Smut Story archive on his behalf, if Eva would accept it. He was very ill, and prone to rambling towards the end, so these could simply be the dementia-fuelled inventions of a dying man. Nonetheless, I have delivered — along with the letter and the tape — my own half of the DNA evidence required to verify at least one part of my father's story. The rest is up to Eva.

[18] Take Peter's story, for instance. It has been added to the archive, and you can ask for it by name. I have listened to it several times now, with Eva. Now it's your turn. Take it, listen, and find out for yourself. There is no knowing how it will strike you. You might turn it into a joke. Or dismiss it. But know that for one person at least, if only for a moment, it was true.

Long before I met Candas in person, I was blown away by her writing. By the stories, characters, and sentences, of course, but also by the sheer diversity of perspectives encompassed by her work. In Black Wine *alone, I encountered a dozen varieties of love, marriage, sex, and family—from utopian to abusive to revolutionary, from monogamous to non-monogamous to monogamish, and various combinations thereof—all in such heterogeneous cultural and personal contexts as to defy easy summary. In a Candas Jane Dorsey novel, sex is never just one thing, even within (or for) a single character, and this sexual diversity stood in vivid contrast to the "normative" culture(s) I was more familiar with, both from the broader world around me and the (relatively) progressive, feminist, pacifist, and social-justice-oriented Mennonite subculture in which I was raised.[19] Like the work of Ursula K. Le Guin or Samuel R. Delaney, Candas's writing opened up whole new worlds of possibility, new ways of thinking and being. I was entranced. And yet, when I tried to write an SF story about the odd juxtaposition of sexual pleasure and guilt in contemporary North American contexts, I found myself stuck. Until I returned to Candas's essay, "Being One's Own Pornographer," which supplied the epigraph for this story. And somehow, magically, that cracked the whole thing open so it could start coming together. (So to speak.) I can't easily explain all the ways Candas's writing has influenced mine since I first read—and then reread, and reread again—her work. But this story might be a good start.*

---

[19] Briefly: Yes, we had electricity and TV. No, we didn't travel by horse and buggy.

CANDAS OF BOYLE STREET

One summer day in 2013, Candas Jane Dorsey and her partner Timothy Anderson arrived at our house in the Highlands (Edmonton) to pick up a compost bin and miscellaneous gardening supplies. I had known them both for at least 30 years, from a distance, because of their successful careers as local artists. But I distinctly remember thinking at the time, "What great people!"

The reason for their visit was a major downsizing project I was immersed in. My husband's loss of mobility had required us to move to an apartment with elevators and no stairs.

A few months later we had managed to resettle in a highrise apartment, Riverside Towers, on 86 Street and Jasper Avenue. Having been an engaged resident of the Highlands for almost 25 years, I wondered what new community I had landed in. I looked on the City of Edmonton website and was rather dismayed to learn that the answer was "Boyle Street." For decades, many Edmontonians including me have viewed Boyle Street with suspicion, associating it with a slum-like environment and fairly extreme urban challenges related to poverty, racism, mental health issues and more.

That fall I discovered that Candas was running for city council in our ward and offered to deliver her brochures to the people of Riverside Towers, which has approximately 300 apartments. When I went to pick up the brochures at Candas' house, I learned that she lived only a few blocks away from me.

I am not sure exactly how things evolved after that. But when the election was over (she lost), Candas and I found ourselves keeping regular Monday morning appointments to get some exercise by going for a walk. As it turned out, the walks were perhaps not so much fitness pursuits—although there was certainly some of that—as tours of the hood and noodles at Pagolac on 97 Street and other nearby restaurants.

Candas took it upon herself to show me the wonders of the diverse, historic and densely populated Boyle Street community. She helped me to see that there is truly no other neighbourhood like it in this city. And I mean that in a good way.

The residents include significant numbers of Aboriginal and Chinese residents, along with newcomers from numerous countries around the world, older people like me who have chosen apartment living in retirement and young people who wish to live close to downtown.

I learned that the location is wonderful for me, a senior who is still active. Boyle Street is within easy walking distance of City Hall and Churchill Square, City Centre Mall, arts venues such as the Winspear Centre and Citadel Theatre, and much more, including Little Italy and Chinatown. Candas and I visited many of these places on our walks and on other outings.

Boyle Street is the location of several services for marginalized and homeless people. Yes, there are bottle pickers with carts, enclaves of homeless campers in good weather and service agencies such as the Mustard Seed that feeds people. Yes, some of the community events involve barbecues with long line-ups of people who are excited to get some free food.

There are also historic buildings constructed during the very beginnings of the city, since Boyle Street was the original downtown area of Edmonton. It moved west only after the Hudson's Bay Company sold its land west of 97 Street.

A description of this community is a whole other story, but these details serve to illustrate what Candas did for me. She helped me to make this area a home where I feel comfortable walking about and one that I am proud of instead of feeling embarrassed to tell people where I live.

I doubt that Candas did this out of charity, but rather because she herself is a true citizen of Boyle Street herself. She was very active in the building of the beautiful Boyle Street Plaza at 95 Street and 103A Avenue, and she has invited me to get involved with the Boyle Street Community League.

We may not be able to live here for as long as we would like. But each day and week of our residence here, coming on to five years now, has been enhanced by the knowledge that I have a friend and neighbour named Candas Jane Dorsey.

Many of the articles and essays submitted for this project will be about Candas' writing life. But it is important for people to know that she is also a committed social activist who has contributed a great deal in that area as well.

FLASH FICTIONS

Afternoon Break

It only seems like it's always full-moon night at the Tesseract. Even in broad daylight.

I was on the first week of my three weeks allotment of vacation time at the paper. So, early Friday afternoon, I dropped by the pub for a half-pint before taking in one of the matinees at the Mayfair. I was thinking maybe the latest Avengers or else something animated.

Ernie and Raj were at the corner chess table, studying the board. Sky and the Hobbit hovered over them, critiquing the game and offering advice on moves. A few other regulars occupied tables, enjoying a quiet afternoon glass while chatting or just contemplating the air.

Perched on my own stool at the end of the bar, I watched as Shale slowly drew off my mug full of Wolfshead draft. He was just picking up the steel ruler to swipe off the foam when the front door banged open.

Everyone looked up, squinting at the bright high-noon rectangle of light. In through the door, out of Vancouver's July heatwave, rushed this manic-looking guy, dressed up in what I guess you might call Mad Max modern, complete to a pair of goggles shoved up high on his forehead.

Wild eyes stared around the room. Fixed on Shale, standing behind the bar.

"Quick!" he shouted. "What year is this?"

Shale answered without a moment's hesitation. "It's 2014, dude."

The stranger stomped a foot and cursed. "Damn it! Calibration's still off!"

He spun around and, still muttering loudly about "temporal vectors" and "coding glitches", stomped back out the door and disappeared into the sidewalk traffic.

We all watched as the door slowly swung shut. Blinked our eyes and then went back to what we were doing before the interruption. I turned to find Shale just finishing flicking the foam off the ruler while at the same time handing over my half-pint mug.

He looked back over towards the door and shook his head.

"Third time this year," he said with a shrug.

Good Eatin'

Hey there, folks! Mad Melford here with another steal of a deal. I guarantee there's lots of good eatin' waiting here for you.

Now Thanksgiving is just around the corner. And we all know what that means, right? You got it. Turducken!

I dunno 'bout you, but to me nothin' says Thanksgiving in America more than a chicken stuffed inside a duck shoved up nice and tight inside of a big ol' butterball turkey, with everythin' just swimming in rich gravy inside a hot roasting pan.

But Melford, you say, we're all as crazy about turducken as the next guy, but even one of them just ain't enough to feed all the family come to call for Thanksgiving at our house.

I understand, folks, I do indeed, I've been there myself, yessir. Well, not to worry, my friends, because we here at Mad Melford's Maniacal Merchandising—take Interstate 12 to the Wilbanks off-ramp—have got the answer to your problem in just one simple word.

Dodoturducken.

Yessir, we have embraced the miracle of mad science to find the solution to your Thanksgiving holiday menu dilemma. Thanks to the wonders of reverse genetic engineering, plus a little dash of recombinant DNA for good measure, we have the perfect main course for your Thanksgiving meal plan. For a price so low we are practically giving it away, you get a nice free-range chicken nestled inside a plump mallard slipped inside a corn-fed butterball turkey, and all that meaty goodness stuffed inside a gen-u-wine prime fresh-from-the-factory dodo. That's a good 50 pounds at least of all-American birds ready for roasting inside the oven or sticking on a spit for barbecue. And that comes with my personal guarantee, folks, that your dodo is mutation-free. Yessir, not a trace of cellular degeneration or any tainted DNA. I dare you to find a single out-of-place mitochondria in your dodoturducken. Cross-my-heart-swear-to-God double-your-money-back if I'm lyin'.

But if you've got a big, and I mean monster-sized, family reunion coming up, or maybe you're just the friendly sort likes to invite the whole neighbourhood over for Thanksgiving barbecue, we here at Mad Melford's are taking orders in advance right now for our "Big Bird" specials, like dodoturducken-stuffed Australian ostrich. Not enough, you say? Well, how about our exclusive Giant Moa Meal Deal? Just bustin' out all over with plenty of dodoturducken.

And for the football crowd out there—you know who you are—give us just one week's advance notice and we will deliver to your door one fully-packed Elephant Bird, crammed full of dodoturducken and ready for the luau pit. I recommend a good chainsaw when it's time to carve into your aepyornis. Tell you one thing, folks, there will be NO arguments over the drumsticks with this baby.

Remember, folks, that's Mad Melford's Maniacal Merchandising, we're open 24-seven, so get on that phone right now to 1-888-MELFORD. You can also email us at Mad4Melford@hotmail.com. Or just come on down and say hello, we're at the Mobi Strip Mall in beautiful downtown Escherville. Oh, and bring the kiddies too, 'cause we got lollipops for all of them and a genuine pushmepullyu to ride around on while you browse around, maybe even get your auto-graphed picture taken with our guest celebrity, Morgo the Friendly Grelb.

Remember, folks, that's Mad Melford's Maniacal Merchandising. Where mad science is not just the answer to everything, it's a way of life!

Now stay tuned for *Creature Feature Classic Theatre* featuring mud-wrestling at its finest in *Bride of Frankenstein versus Dracula's Daughter*, back-to-back with *Gidget Goes Gaga with Gorgo*!

Jimmy Smith Has a Dinosaur

"Moooooommmmm! Pleeeeease?"

"No, Billy, you can't have one."

Billy's mom picked up another plate, one of the chipped ones, and started wiping it dry with quick, almost-savage strokes of the dishtow-el. She knew what was coming next.

"But why, mom?" argued Billy. "Jimmy Smith has a dinosaur!"

Billy's mom sighed. Put the plate in the cupboard, reached for an-other, began wiping it dry. "If Jimmy Smith's parents choose to let him have a dinosaur, that is their decision and they can afford to do so. Me, I really don't think it's proper to let a child have that kind of a pet."

Even if it is "just a micro-sized plant-eater" like that Amelia said.

"But mooooooommmmmm!"

"Don't "but mom!" me!" Billy's mom spat. "No dinosaur and that is final!"

Billy scuffed a sneaker-clad foot against a crack in the kitchen linoleum. "S'not fair. Jimmy Smith gets to have a dinosaur, he gets to ride around on his own SeaSkidoo, gets to learn kickboxing with Jackie Chan's clone, go to Mars for summer holidays, to…"

"Oh, for pity's sake!" Billy's mom cried in exasperation. "If Jimmy Smith got permission to jump off a cliff, would you want to go too?"

Blessed silence followed. For a moment. Then…

"Jimmy Smith has a jetpack."

Candas Jane Dorsey became part of my "nationalist Canadian sf" phase several decades ago when I learned that there was such a thing as Canadian science fiction, and that Canadian sf had a definite difference of opinion and point of view from American and British sf. While I never had actual contact, either in person or by correspondence, with Dorsey to receive any mentoring or advice, her own short fiction, as in her collection, Machine Sex and Other Stories, taught me that "off the wall" works very well for sf themes, plots and story ideas. That has been her greatest influence on me and my writing.

SAMI'S SONG

The night air reeked of magic. The stench came over the foothills, carried on a warm southern wind, filling our town with a scent as obvious to the nose as fog is to the eyes. When dawn came, all of Elric Bane's chickens were eaten, and he was left to dispose of the carcasses. It seemed that for the first time in five years a beast had come.

That morning my father cooked breakfast. As we sat, the remnants of our meal still on the table, finishing our tea together he said, "There's a good story in this one, Sami."

"Are you feeling inspired?" I asked.

He smiled. "No, I will have to see how it turns out. Maybe this one is yours."

The back of my neck prickled. I was eighteen and had not yet proven myself in combat, three years past the time I should've had a challenger. Our town had been a remarkably peaceful place for the past five years. My fifteenth birthday had arrived with no challenger, a disappointment but also a relief. However, the longer time wore on, the more anxious I felt about ever being a capable warrior when my time came. Besides, songs composed by bards were inspired by glorious deaths, and I did not aspire to such a fate.

That afternoon my father took a long walk. His long grey hair was tied back, and his jaw was clenched slightly in determination. I knew that he would wander far from town, composing his next story. There was a celebration coming—the Festival of the Blood Moon—and as the town bard he needed a story to tell, a great one. There were many he could draw from, but he wanted something new.

I didn't inherit my father's talent for music and words. Nor, it seemed, did I inherit my mother's strength either. I was scrawny, even though I was eighteen. My father said my strength was wiry and quick, rather than brawn as my mother's had been. Her armour lay in a trunk at the foot of my father's bed, waiting for me, though I was certain there was no way my shoulders would ever fill the generous iron plate, nor would my arms ever be able to lift that sword.

As my father walked I examined her armour. I never looked at it when he was around. I pulled the shoulder guards and the chain mail out, so heavy that I wondered how anyone managed to wear them. The mail was tarnished from many years of disuse, and I took a soft cloth and rubbed away the grime covering the image on the chest plate: a heart, surrounded by a sun, my family crest. At one time the crest had been crimson and gold, now the colours were scratched and dull. Below the crest, was a large hole, the metal smooth where it had been punctured and forced inward. A large hole where the griffin's claw had torn through the thick plate.

My father came back from his wander, but he didn't look relaxed as he usually did after a good walk.

"Any good ideas come to you?" I asked, just to make conversation.

"No, there's something out there. I couldn't concentrate." He sat down on a chair and massaged his temples. "The Blood Moon is in ten days. I'm not sure what I'll do."

"You could always sing…" I began

"*Gerti's Song?*" he finished, correctly anticipating what I was going to say. "They've heard it before, far too many times."

I didn't reply. I loved *Gerti's Song*, the ballad my father had written for my mother after her death. As a child my father sang it to me almost every night, though I often fell asleep before the end. When he tried to tell me other stories or sing other songs, I would protest until he came around. It was true though, he had sung *Gerti's Song* many times. And though everyone listened rapturously when he sang, many would talk of how he still loved my mother too much and what a pity it was that he never remarried. There was one person, in particular, who resented his choice to remain a widower.

The next day, after another restless night thick with magic, all of Balaeric Heber's goats were gone. The day after, all the village cats disappeared.

The third night of loss proved to be the last straw. The following evening Andi, the village elder, called all citizens to council.

Andi was a tall and exceptionally beautiful woman. Though her years of fighting were behind her, her past was evident in her well-muscled arms, still toned though many years had passed. Tonight she wore the light-blue robes of the village elder. Though she was not the oldest person in the town, she was admired for her intelligence and wise council. However, she was no friend to me. For years Andi had tried to persuade my father to marry her. It had begun shortly after my mother died, and my father had been, and remained, obstinate in his refusal.

"A beast lurks nearby, using dark magic to steal our animals stealthily in the night," Andi began. "For three years we have enjoyed peace and prosperity in our village. However, because of this some of our women remain untested in combat. But the time has come for the next recruit to prove herself." Andi turned to a small hunched man who held a scroll in his hand. "Master Elric, who is the next warrior to come of age? Who shall challenge this beast?"

Before he finished unrolling the scroll, I and everyone else in the village knew what he would say. "Sami Gertidoter," he announced, in his thin, wavering voice.

All eyes turned to me, including Andi, whose smile lifted a bit in the corner of her mouth. "Is that so?" she said. "In that case, you will begin training tomorrow with Champion Raini. You have three days to prepare. The matter is urgent."

I looked around at all the village folk watching me, critiquing my thinness, my small arms, my weak shoulders. Their gazes said it all: this is our hero?

Then I met my father's eyes, and his expression was crushing. His lips were pursed thin, neither smiling nor frowning, but his eyes were sorrowful. We had both known this moment would come, yet it seemed that neither of us were prepared.

Champion Raini was an esteemed warrior, still young but childless, and part of the midnight guard. I had trained with her when I was younger, but after my fifteenth birthday came and went we stopped the lessons and I focused on working the farm.

My father was a respected bard but a mediocre farmer. With the termination of my training I was responsible for plowing and sowing the fields, caring for our flock of chickens, and maintaining the vege-table garden. I was still skinny, but strong enough for these tasks, and found in myself an affinity for the work. I had planned on expanding and soon adding goats to our farm, but everything would now be put on hold.

That night I instructed my father on how to care for our land. "The chicken feed is stored along the eaves, away from water, and most importantly, away from the chickens," I said. He nodded limply as I continued. "Check the field every day for rot and for signs of animals. Bring in the crops a few days before the Harvest Moon. Then you'll beat everyone else to market."

He looked at me with alarm as I said this. "Surely you'll be back in time to take care of that."

"Maybe," I said, with little expression in my voice.

My training began, and Raini did her best. By the end of the first day I could lift and move my sword. The second day we practiced striking and dodging. Slowly my combat education returned to me, though my armour was dented from Raini's blows.

"Good job Challenger," she said to me that evening. "See you to-morrow."

Though I tried to hide it, my lip trembled, and Raini saw. "Sami," she said, putting her mailed hand on my shoulder. "Fear is natural, but it can either give us power or sap our strength. I know you're scared, but this is what you have been raised to do."

My arms hung heavily at my side. I didn't want to cry in front of her, but the tears came unbidden. I said nothing, for fear that a sob would escape me, and when I gained control of myself I finally said, "I am not strong enough to do this."

Raini snorted. "Not every beast is defeated by brute strength. You are fast and you are smart. Remember that."

I tried to let Raini's words lift my spirits. I had little time to think on it—that night I fell into an exhausted, dreamless sleep.

On the evening after my third day of training, my father cooked for me my favourite meal: sweet small brown trout that had been stewed with tomatoes until they were so soft you could eat the fish whole. I ate with gusto despite my nerves—my appetite was incredible since I had begun training.

That night my body ached all over. I lay under my scratchy blanket, and tried not to focus on how my muscles twitched and throbbed. Before I blew out my lamp, my father came in.

He kissed my forehead. "Goodnight my sweet Sami."

"Good night Papa," I said, and then I asked, "can you sing me mother's song?"

He smiled. "Of course."

He started then, and sang in a quiet voice that was full of love. He sang of her beautiful golden braid that usually hung over one shoulder, but how her hair was shorn short for combat. He sang of her flashing blue eyes and ruddy cheeks, her strong arms and broad chest. He sang of her sword, *Griffinbane*, the sword that would be mine tomorrow.

And then finally, he sang of her bravery, how with her dying strength she plunged her sword into the heart of the griffin who had impaled her with his claw. An honourable death, the kind they will sing of for ages to come.

"Thank you," I said when he finished.

"I love you," he said softly. I saw the deep crease in his forehead and his tired eyes, and hoped my father would not have to write a song about me.

The next day I was up with the sunrise. I ate substantially, knowing that I would need the strength if I hoped to survive. My father rose early too, and after I finished breakfast he said he had something for me.

I followed him to his chamber, and spread out on his bed was my mother's armour. Links had been removed to shorten the tunic and bring the shoulders closer together. The hole under the breastplate had been mended so handily that only I would know that the metal had a slightly different sheen. Best of all, our family crest seemed to glow crimson and gold, heat seeming to radiate from the heart and the sun.

My father lifted *Griffinbane*, which lay beside the armour. He took my braid in one hand and with the other deftly cut it from my scalp. It lay on the floor like a serpent, not golden like my mother's but brown, some colour between her hair and my father's black that had many years before turned grey.

"It's time," he said. I slid the mail tunic on and then the shoulder and breastplate on top. I donned my shin guards, the plates along my arms and my helmet. It felt strange without my braided hair underneath, but it fit snugly to my head now.

My mail tunic made a shivering sound as I left the room. Out of the corner of my eye, I saw my father collect my braid and place it on his bed.

"Its lair is near here," said Andi, gesturing to the large hill in front of us. It couldn't be far—the acrid stink of its magic filled the air, and I couldn't imagine how the stench could possibly get any stronger.

Andi turned to me, smiling, but her eyes were cold. "Good luck Challenger," she said.

With that, I was dismissed. I turned my back on Andi and the procession that had led me out of the town. The town had been silent when I left; no one cheered from the windows. The night before a newborn baby had disappeared, a little girl. This was a solemn loss to the community—she was the only girl born so far this year, the only hope for a future warrior. The windows and doors had been shut tight, as if that could keep the magic and the beast out.

Alone, I stumbled along, feeling myself begin to sweat under the weight of my armour. The scent of magic grew stronger until I found a deep hole in the side of a hill. It was remarkable that the hill still stood with such a cavernous chunk missing, but such is the power of magic. I unsheathed *Griffinbane* and entered.

Two steps in, the darkness enveloped me completely, and panic flooded my chest. The darkness felt smothering, like a wet blanket and I had trouble breathing. Yet I continued, inching my way forward.

Then suddenly I heard it: "Ssssssss." A long, low hiss. I froze. The noise was soft but resonant, coming from something large. My monster.

I felt something near my foot and I jerked back, but too late. Something coiled around my ankle. In my fear I tried to turn and run and instead fell, *Griffinbane* falling from my hand and landing with a sharp clang against a rock.

Whatever had me by the foot dragged me backwards, and I clawed at the dirt floor of the cave, desperate for my survival, more afraid than I had ever been. I did not want to see it. I could not seem to regain my senses from the panic, and when the coils crept up my body, I fought to control my breathing. They squeezed and I cried out, expelling all air from my lungs.

"Ssssoooo…you have come to me," the creature said, but not with any voice of this world. It spoke directly into my head.

I made a little noise then, a sort of rasp, and the coils loosened so that I could breathe. With my sword gone, I couldn't credibly declare that I was there to kill the beast, but if it could speak, perhaps it could understand my words too. I could at least beg.

"Please, let me go," I said in a weak voice.

"Why? So you can crawl back to your people like the worm you are? I know you have been sent to kill me, but you cannot." Two glowing eyes opened in front of me, pale yellow with slit pupils in the middle. The light that emanated from its eyes revealed a large flat head with smooth scales, each the size of my hand.

"You're a snake," I said.

"Hmph, a ssssnake," it said in disgust. "No mere snake, my lady. I am a bócwyrm, the sworn guardian of the king's library. Since his death I have had to make my home elsewhere and your village is a good place for a creature like me."

Its coils had loosened more, and I thought that if it kept talking, perhaps it would become distracted and loosen them further, or even let me slip away.

"Why are you here?" I asked.

"Ssstories," the bócwyrm said. "There is a bard here who tells good stories. It is the only way I can rest. I feed on stories."

"The bard is my father," I said.

"Really?" exclaimed the bócwyrm, tightening his coils around me for a moment. "I heard him the other day as he walked by my cave. He was creating a fantastic tale, absolutely delicious."

"Delicious?" I said.

"Yes, stories nourish me. I eat them," said the bócwyrm. "But sadly, once I eat a story it is gone forever—the teller will not remember the tale ever again. That is why I must eat other things too, though I do prefer a story."

I remembered how my father came back from his wander without a story planned for the Blood Moon. Had the bócwyrm eaten it, then?

"Tell me a story, my lady, if you are the child of this bard. I will spare your precious village if you will tell me stories."

"Alright," I said, "But I can barely breathe. Let me go."

"After your story you may leave, but if you don't come back tomorrow night, I will eat another girl from your village. I will work my way from youngest to oldest, and then move on to the men." With that, the bócwyrm loosened its grip and removed its coils, leaving only a thin coil of its tail looped around my foot.

My heart pounded. I tried to think through the stories my father had told. I remembered parts, but others seemed to slip from my grasp, and compounded by my nervous state I could barely remember even stories that had seemed so familiar to me.

"I'm growing bored, my lady," said the bócwyrm.

"I have one," I said.

"Go on."

I began the story, a rough retelling of a ballad my father often sang of doomed lovers, Ani and Taeric, whose families disapproved of their love. It ended with Ani throwing herself off a cliff into the sea and Taeric dying of heartbreak on the sand, which is why the waves rush to the shore, and then cling to the sand as they are pulled away by the ocean, as the water pulled Ani away from Taeric. Of course, I couldn't sing like my father, but when I was done the bócwyrm sat for a moment in silence.

"Is that all?" it asked.

"Yes, that's the end."

"Sssomewhat sssatisfying," it said. "I grow weary, my lady, and I will sleep for now. Tomorrow you ought to have a better story. That one was merely acceptable." The coil unwound from around my calf, and with a hiss, the bócwyrm slithered further into the darkness.

I scrambled out of the cave as fast as I could, glad to be able to breathe the fresh air, tainted with the stink of magic as it was, it was still the air of freedom.

Freedom. For now.

I ran at first towards the village, and then realized I could not return home without the certainty that the village was safe. That would be as good as defeat, returning empty-handed. I would have to slay the bócwyrm, but my sword lay somewhere in the oppressive darkness of the cave. I had a day to think of something. But first, I had to think of my next story.

As the bócwyrm had said, I remembered nothing of the story I had told it, only that it had seemed dissatisfied. I tried to remember my father's better tales, and finally settled on one about a lonely man who falls in love with his scarecrow, who comes alive at night. Once his neighbours discover the man dancing in the moonlight with his animated scarecrow, they burn it. The man saves a bit of straw from the scarecrow before it burns and sleeps with it under his pillow. Meanwhile, the Queen of the land must take a husband, and she goes from house to house asking each man to give her his most prized possession in order for her to help judge his character. When the lonely man gives her the straw and tells her his tale, the Queen is charmed by his devotion and chooses to marry him, since he values true love over all.

I passed the rest of the day and night out in the hills, huddled on the lea side of the hill when the cold winds came at night. I practiced the story, remembering the cadences of my fathers' voice, his gesticulations, his blazing blue eyes and enchanting expressions. I tried my best to imitate them, knowing that I fell far short of his skill. It would have to do.

As the next day dawned, I made my way back to the cave. "I'm here, bócwyrm," I called. While I waited for a response, I groped around the floor of the cave trying to find my sword, with no luck.

"Aaaaah," sighed the bócwyrm. "You have returned. Well, let's hear it."

I launched into the story, and told it with as much gusto as I could manage. The bócwyrm listened—despite not being able to see it I could feel its rapt attention on me.

When I finished, the bócwyrm sighed again. "Very good, but I tire of these tales of love. I used to live in a castle, you know. I wish for a tale of adventure. Tomorrow though, for I grow very tired after such a meal." Once again, the coil unwound from my leg, and the bócwyrm disappeared into the dark.

The relief I felt afterwards was tremendous. I had exhausted myself in the telling of the story, and I curled up at the mouth of the cave, unable to travel very far, and slept.

I awoke in the evening, anxiety gnawing at the pit of my stomach. I remembered the bócwyrm's wishes for a story of adventure, and I tried to recall any. None came to mind. None that is, other than my mother's tale, *Gerti's Song*.

I couldn't sing it to the bócwyrm. The song was the only memory I had of my mother—I had been too young when she died to know anything else about her. Yet the more I tried to think, the fewer stories I remembered until my mother's song was all that filled my mind.

I spent a restless evening in the hills, oblivious to my own hunger and thirst, the provisions I'd brought with me long consumed. I listened to the wind wail and felt it tear at my face and whip around my shorn hair. I had plenty of time to think of my utter failure as a warrior, and yet as the sun finally rose I felt a sort of resolution within me. I would give the bócwyrm my mother's story. It was all I had to give, but it was the most powerful thing I owned.

I stood up and entered the cave. I left my helm at the door, and my heavy armour. For some reason, I felt that I would not need it.

"Bócwyrm," I called. "I have my very best story for you."

A low hiss came from the back of the cave, and its yellow eyes opened near me. In the dim light I could see it was coiled up comfortably, its eyes fixed on me, ready for my story.

This one I could sing. Though my voice was thin and warbly at best, when I sang my mother's song I sang with gusto. I sang of her pure love and kind heart, of her bravery and love of her people. I sang of her donning her mail to rid the village of the griffin that had already killed the previous champion. I sang of her nameless sword, and how she stood on her two strong legs and defied the griffin. I sang of its scream of rage and how my mother fought and dodged the beast for many hours, severing its leg and bloodying its beak. Still it fought on and with a missing leg it took to flying. I sang of how it came silently from the trees and pinned her to the ground, piercing her with its one remaining talon. Hot tears burned from my eyes yet my voice stayed strong as I sang of her dying sword thrust, straight and true into the heart of the griffin.

I sang of the village's sorrow, of the peace that reigned for two years afterwards, and how her sword was named *Griffinbane* by the village elder and preserved for her only daughter, the daughter who would take up her mantle.

My voice grew quiet as I reached the end, and every word seemed to burn in my throat as they left me one by one forever.

When the last note rang out, I waited to hear the bócwyrm's critique. Instead, I heard nothing. I sat there, my heart empty, my only remaining memory the fact that I once knew a song about my mother, but that I would never again know the words.

Tears flowed from my eyes still, and I tried to collect myself. I heard a soft sigh from in front of me, and I realized that I could not see the bócwyrm's eyes. It was sound asleep.

I could run, I thought, and then I dismissed the thought immediately. This creature had taken my mother's story from me. I had to end it.

I crawled backwards, away from the bócwyrm, as quietly as I could. As I moved I grew angrier and angrier. When I tried to recall my mother, not a single memory came, and in fact, the word mother seemed to become abstract entirely. As though other people had mothers, but not me, not ever. And this thought enraged me, because I knew I was missing something indescribably important but I did not know what it was. This creature had taken my mother from me.

It was then that my hand hit something cool and smooth. It made a clattering sound as my hand pushed it into the rocks. I pulled my hand away as though I had been burned.

Carefully, I groped around until my hand grasped the familiar shape of a hilt. I had found my sword. I stood up, and inched to the side, both hands on the hilt now.

As I circled the bócwyrm, I was grateful I had removed my noisy mail. I was grateful for my small quick stature that made it easy to manoeuvre through the cave. And I was grateful for the blade in my hands.

I could not see the head of the bócwyrm, yet I knew what I needed to do: I needed to cut off its head in one swift motion to make my own survival more likely. In order to accomplish this, I would need to wake the beast for the light of its yellow eyes and then make my move as quickly as possible.

Once I was in a position that I thought would put me beside the bócwyrm's neck, I drew in a deep breath. With my foot, I nudged the coiled body, and then delivered a swift kick. Nothing, happened. I tried again, and nothing. I bent down and grasped a sharp rock and threw it where I thought the bócwyrm's head would be.

There was a hollow thud followed by the appearance of two angry yellow slits.

"Playing gamesss, my lady?" the bócwyrm hissed, and I raised my sword, but I was too slow. The eyes disappeared for a moment, and then a great force hit my shoulder, sending me sprawling.

But this time, I held onto my blade.

I rolled onto my back just in time to see two yellow eyes rear up above me. I felt the warm hiss of its breath on my face. Then the eyes plummeted closer, and with a cry that came from the depths of my chest, I swung my sword in a long arc.

My timing was perfect. *Griffinbane*, freshly cleaned and sharpened, cut through the thick neck of the bócwyrm. I felt the shearing of flesh from flesh. It didn't even have time to scream. Its head hit the ground beside me, and I felt a shower of warm blood cover my body.

I lay there for a long time, alarmed and disgusted with what I had done, but exhilarated as well. I had done it. I had completed my first kill; I was a Champion now.

As the exhilaration left my body, I tried to recall what had happened. I had told the bócwyrm a story…of what? It was a story dear to me, that I knew.

I collected the bócwyrm's head, and exited the cave, donning my armour before heading to the village.

Saidi, a young girl of twelve who acted as the village scout, saw me before anyone else did.

"Sami's back!" she cried. "With its *head*!"

By the time I reached the edge of the village, people filled the streets and leaned out of windows, cheering and cheering. They smelled the sweet air and filled their lungs so that they could shout praises at me. I lifted the beast's head, its black forked tongue lolling hideously out of its gaping mouth, revealing two pointed fangs.

I presented the head to the Andi, who ordered it to be preserved and mounted and hung in the town hall, where the heads of all beasts went. She received it gracefully, yet I could sense that perhaps she wished I had been less successful in my endeavor.

Once I could leave the celebrations, my father waited for me at the door of our house, with a warm tub of bathwater and my favourite stewed trout steaming on a plate. He helped me remove my armour, and his brow furrowed when he saw my stained tunic.

"Were you not wearing your mail?" he asked in concern.

"It was too loud," I said.

He shook his head. "You must tell me the whole tale."

"I will later," I said, and he left so I could bathe in privacy.

As I washed, I tried again to remember the tales I had told, but they were gone. I felt a pang of sorrow, yet I was even beginning to lose sense of what exactly I missed.

As promised, I recounted the tale to my father, including the bócwyrm's promise that I would not remember the tales. I could still describe some elements of the tales I told the bócwyrm, but could not recount them in their entirety. He looked concerned at first, but when I reached the third tale, his eyebrows furrowed together so tightly they almost touched.

"You mean you sang the bócwyrm *Gerti's Song*?"

I frowned. "Yes, I think so."

My father put his head in his hands and when he looked up again there were tears in his eyes. "That was the greatest gift I ever gave you, my daughter," he said.

"I'm sorry I lost it," I said.

"No," he said. "Don't be sorry. That story saved your life."

After a moment, I asked him. "Could you try telling it to me again?"

He smiled. "Of course."

My father began to sing, and each word I heard again for the first time, and yet as soon as the song entered my mind it slipped away like sand through an hourglass. It was beautiful, but as soon as my father concluded one sentence, it was gone, and so the story had no continuity.

This I did not tell him, but I think he sensed that I did not enjoy *Gerti's Song* as much as I once had.

The Festival of the Blood Moon drew near, and my father had taken to wandering for hours in the foothills, composing his latest tale. I had resumed my daily chores around the farm. My armour had been cleaned and put away, and I had no desire to take it up again.

Finally, the festival arrived, and after the feast everyone gathered around my father, eagerly anticipating a story. He stood in front of the fire, his features dramatically lit by the dancing flames.

"I have a new composition to share, written for the celebration of this exceptional Blood Moon," he said. He strummed his lute once to check the tuning, and then launched into a rambling set of chords, music that made one think of travelling, the sound of cart wheels on a hard road.

He lifted his chin and sang:

This is the story of Gerti's only daughter
Child of a woman both lovely and strong
In these words hear the pride of her father
Listen as I sing for you Sami's Song

ABOUT CANDAS

Once in a great while we meet someone who, without realizing it, changes our lives forever.

Once upon a time I toyed with the idea that I could be writer. I was long grown before I realized that I could be a writer. My friend Astrid and I used to make up stories for ourselves about kickass women and one day, sitting in her living room drinking copious quantities of coffee, we started just making up a story.

We sat down at my new Sperry "transportable" computer and began writing our adventures. They were ours (as the story was a classic Mary Sue) except we were galactic secret agents. We used all our recent real adventures and conversations, expanded them, made a quiet immigrant family into real aliens, and proceeded to turn Astrid's cat Fred into a character, too. We didn't understand plot, story arc, or theme. We wrote it for laughs, bouncing back and forth gleefully from one head to another—my head, Astrid's head, and every character's head without regard for structured point of view.

Astrid was a fast typist. I mean FAST—she could pound keys faster than her IBM Selectric typewriter could keep up—over 90 words per minute. I plugged along at about 35 words a minute. So I typed, and as she watched the words flow onto the page, she'd make suggestions, speaking into my ear like Odin's ravens.

We spent the summer on and off writing, and we ended up with a very short, but funny novel.

We decided to send it to a couple of publishers. I stapled my business card to the front page, figuring the publishing editors would know it was a cold submission we wanted them to buy and that if they liked it, we didn't need a cover letter. They'd write or call. We didn't even supply a self-addressed stamped envelope because we didn't have any America stamps and didn't know about IRCs. So naïve!

We did send two copies to appropriate New York genre publishers. We got back the entire manuscript from one with a nice rejection letter. The second copy eventually came back, also with a super nice and encouraging rejection letter saying they'd sent the manuscript on to their UK publisher, but it wasn't quite right for either of them.

So, we thought maybe we needed to do some edits; we hadn't really done more than check for spelling.

The amazing Monica Hughes was Writer in Residence at the Edmonton Public Library. She said nice things, but warned it slowed very much in the middle, as if we'd stopped writing for a month or so. That was pretty close to the truth. She didn't comment much more than that.

Then the novel sat on my shelf gathering dust.

The nagging in the back of my head started. I really wanted to write more.

I discovered a non-credit University of Alberta Extension course that ran all day on Saturdays for a month or so. It seemed daunting. Astrid wasn't interested in doing it, so I plucked up my courage and went alone.

There I met Candas Jane Dorsey, the instructor.

She scared me.

Don't get me wrong. She scared me in a good way.

It was soon after that she changed my life.

I'd never met any woman so confident, well-spoken, and knowledgeable who wasn't a jerk or know-it-all. She lacked the arrogance

I'd come to expect from most professorial types. I didn't feel diminished by anything she said or did. She was approachable. She was also ill (non-contagious) and that made being in a very uncomfortable classroom hard for her. She asked us if anyone would object to having the classes in her home. There weren't very many of us and we all agreed. It was far more comfy for us, too.

We had that first class in Corbett Hall—an old brick building from the University's younger days. I can't remember if we brought manuscripts that first day, but I well remember the day Candas gave us our first critiques.

Critiques are wild, crazy things. They can make or break a work, and occasionally make or break a new writer. Depending on how they're delivered, they can sting worse than Portuguese Man-o-War tentacles sliding over exposed skin. Since most writers are fragile things, those crit-tentacles can keep some people away from the writing-beach entirely.

Were it not for the fact that all the words in my manuscript were not mine, and that I could share the good, the bad and the ugly with Astrid, things might have gone a little differently for me. Not having to bear alone the brunt of those tentacles helped.

Candas turned to me.

She scowled.

She scared me more.

Her voice was strong, her words clear and precise. She was angry!

My heart leapt into my throat. I hoped I wouldn't cry.

"….someone with so much obvious talent…"

What?

That's when I started to listen carefully—all thoughts of disaster banished. She severely chastised me for stereotypical characters and clichés in particular. I clung to those words "obvious talent". I could fix clichés. I could fix the stereotypes, and she told me how to do just that.

My assignment for the next class was to take a small section of the work and change the gender of the character. I took it a step farther and changed every one of the characters.

It was great! It was fun!

I could hardly wait for the next class.

She laughed, but I think somewhat shocked I'd done so much. She reminded me she didn't mean the whole thing—just a bit to see the difference.

It was the best lesson writing lesson I ever had.

I stole it for my own use for all kinds of pieces I wrote, and for teaching writing to students and adults alike. I pass that technique on to anyone and everyone I have ever mentored. It's an amazing piece of advice.

That moment changed my life. Candas changed my life. I realised that there really were writers in the world—people who did writerly things for a living. They were people I wanted to know. I wanted to be one of them.

Because of Candas, I have accomplished much and my life is enriched by what she has brought to me, and the people she helped bring into my life. Because of her nothing about my life is the same as it was all those years ago when I sat emotionally cowering in that first class.

Candas is funny, helpful, artistic, talented, loyal, compassionate, one of the smartest people I know, and has lived her life with a pay-it-forward attitude. She was always someone I admired and looked up to. I still admire and look up to her, but now I am honoured to call her a friend. I love her.

Oh yes, and Morris on, you darling Magpie! Happy birthday.

ONE DAY I'M GOING TO GIVE UP THE BLUES FOR GOOD

Little Davis is dead, his body dragged out of the river this dawn. He was murdered, his light snapped out by some jalloo who couldn't let him live for not giving it all. Jalloo. It's a word means client, in our game. Benji made it up one night when she was drunk and high, and it stuck.

Me and Little worked together, down in The Clinic on River Street. The Clinic. To cure what ails you. Whatever it may be. Cure the blues with the Blues, I say. Clinic is the only place you can get the stuff. Little only started working here after he got his habit. Most people, it's where we got ours. But not poor Little. He had me to fuck him up.

Royally.

I come in to work tonight, even though Frankie tell me to stay home. I come in to sit in this chair, soft and grey and comfortable. I come in to look out this window, out onto the street, where I keep hoping I'll see Little dance around the corner, swing into the big glass doors to start shift. But I know he won't.

Because he's dead.

Outside, the blue CLINIC sign blinks off and on, its reflection flashing in the puddles below. The Clinic.

Everything begins here. Here is where it all ends.

At home his ghost sits on the stool under the factory windows, watching the ships on the river, looking for my face in the night crowds below.

But he won't find it.

Because I'm here.

And because ghosts never find each other.

I am a ghost now, and the Blues have all of me, when nothing, and no one should ever have all.

All the time you think it's you that wants the drugs, when really it's the drugs that want you.

They got me now.

Benji comes in, on break from her case. She dances with herself, in front of the mirror. She sings.

"Who do you love?"

"Little Davis," I say, even though I know it's just a song she likes. Outside, the streetlight winks red.

Tells me he's dead.

Benji goes to the fridge, takes out two beers, brings me one. I suck on it, set it down next to the other, stare at the window.

She brings me her kimono, drapes it around my shoulders. "You'll catch your death," she says, and I think, no, I can't, I already caught someone else's. The kimono is turquoise, with dragons embroidered in silver and gold. Benji is beautiful: half black and half Italian. She wears her hair in long dreads; they dance around her pale thin face like dragons. Her dancing hair makes the room go quiet, all still like before the thunderclap. The stillness wraps around me, a second kimono. In my head I thank her for it. Out loud I say:

"Me and Little was gonna quit this year, give up the Blues for good. I don't know what to give up now."

Benji comes over, opens my mouth ever so gently, rests a cigarette between my lips.

I smoke it, thinking it doesn't matter if you die of cancer when you can't feel.

"I used to be able to feel," I say to Benji

"How could you tell?" she asks, dancing

I remember the last time, but I can't talk about it to Benji. I couldn't even talk about it to Little. So I tell her about the time before that. "When Marianne left it felt like I was torn open and my guts pulled out and spread all over the floor and stepped on."

Benji laughs, and I can't really blame her.

Marianne is the first lover I ever lived with, and the only one, besides Little. I would say she was my first lover but she wasn't. She was the first one that counted. "But was it love?"

"My hands shook all the time. The skin under my eyes went grainy, like a photograph that's been blown up too much. Like those."

Wet rings on them now, from my beer bottles. Prints of the body they drug out of the river. But blown up too much. The eyes look bad.

"Don't look at those, Ruby. That's asking for it."

The cops brought them in for identification purposes. I could identify them, all right. No, officer, that's not my sweetheart. My sweetie was beautiful, and what you got there is a piece of meat, all swelled up and ugly. Cops got no sense of humour. Benji fishes around in her stuff, piled up in the corner beside the mirror. She makes her piles of stuff wherever she goes, says it makes her feel at home. I wish I could do that. Feel at home.

"You got an itch to look at pictures, you look at this one."

She kneels on the floor beside me, showing me the postcard. I look down at it. It's a photograph of a lot full of gravel, raked around a pile of rocks.

"So," I say.

"It's a garden. Chuckie sent it to me. It's called Ryōan-ji, and it's in Japan. That's where he went."

"It's a dead quiet kind of place, Benji."

"Quiet, maybe, but no more dead than you right now."

"I wish it was me and not him. You know we were going to Japan? Right after we gave up the Blues. His buddy in Kyoto had a place for us to stay. The one who sends him oranges. You know Little was part Japanese."

"Yeah," says Benji, dancing. "I know." She turns around, dances to me now instead of the mirror. "Too bad it wasn't the right part."

"Yeah. Too bad."

I know she is dancing for me. To make me still, like Chuckie's garden. I wonder whether Benji can still feel, or whether all of her has learned this stillness.

I stare out the window.

It was last Christmas. He was dancing on a table, juggling oranges. He wasn't wearing anything, and he was covered head to toe in silver body paint. He looked maybe seventeen. Later I learned he was twenty, but it was too late; by then he'd already made me feel old.

It was afternoon, the Ocean Club. I'd gone there to try and shake off this case that had left me more spooked than I'd been in years. Since Marianne. It's an arty bar—people who go there have weird hair and no money; they sit around a lot, waiting for life to turn dangerous on them. Because I never waited the Ocean is a kind of vacation for me, and last Christmas it was as far away a place as I could think of from where I'd just been, the chamber of horrors that was my jalloo's mind.

Little ended his song by tossing his oranges into the crowd. There were six of them and the last one he kept for me. When I caught it he smiled. There are smiles, and then there are smiles. Little had the second kind. I got up and followed him into the dressing room. Eyes followed me all the way there, but I didn't mind; I liked the feel of them, tickling my neck.

He was sitting on a stool at the makeup mirror, just lighting up a joint. I closed the door behind me, sat down on the other one, peeled the orange. It's a trick I use on my jalloos: nonchalance gives me the upper hand.

"Mandarins," he said, passing me the number. "From Japan. I got a buddy there sends them to me every Christmas."

So we both knew the same game. I laughed. It was a beginning.

We smoked, ate mandarins. I wanted to sit there all afternoon, basking in his beauty. He was so beautiful: thin, slight even, his body still a boy's, legs dangling from the stool, graceful and bony. His black hair was cropped close to the skull, showing off his Asian cheekbones. The Ocean is a dive; its dressing rooms are tatty: torn leopard upholstery with the foam bulging out. At River Street even the walls are broad-loomed. It gets stifling. I liked the peeling paint, the bare bulb; they set him off, made me want him more. Made me want his startling blue eyes. More.

His smile made me happy to be alive; after this case, a scarce feeling, hopelessly precious. I wanted so bad to make him feel the same way. I wanted so bad for him to like me, but I didn't think he could, ever, like someone like me.

So I reached for the only way I knew would work for sure. Unzipped the pouch on my belt, took the little packet out. Poured blue powder out in a little heap onto the shelf under the mirror.

"Merry Christmas," I said.

A jalloo like my father. Like him, a child molester. Like the leftover bits, the ones I couldn't kill. The bits of memory I couldn't wipe, no matter how long I worked Clinic, how long I lived the Blues. There's not many of them left, those daughter fuckers, thanks in part to us, to the Clinics. But the ones that don't get to us before they go bad, get sent to us after. Except this one just walked in off the street. He headed straight for me, like he was special ordered. They fit me like a glove, all his fuckups.

And so we worked it out.

Like my dad, he'd woken up one day, one eye at least. Taken a look around and realized it was not too cool, what he'd once been up too. Thought he could fix it, and in the worst way. He even found the creep who'd sell him the gun. But on his way home, this wiseacre passes The Clinic, like he does every day of his life. Only this time, something twigs and he comes walking in, straight into my waiting arms. Just lucky, I guess. I was probably the only one in the world who could fix him, aside from his daughter, and you can count her out.

Only to be of any help to him, I had to unlock all my boxes, and they were glued mighty shut. Yanking all those rusty nails out cost me more than it did him. It cost him too, but by the end of the week he'd gained some. He didn't even hate his mother any more. Saw that where her handiwork left off, his had picked up. That surprised him. It always does.

It's like kindergarten, really; making animals out of clay. Just for the hell of it, you think you'll make a monster. Then when clay class is over, you're stuck with it, saying, "Where did this monster come from?" Like you hadn't made it all by your lonesome. But by the end of the week, he'd finally understood. That if you got the itch to make something, there are other things besides monsters. It's not like it's written in the rule book somewhere, that a monster is what you have to make. Only a lot of people see it that way. Some make big monsters, some make little ones. By the end of clay class, you've got one hell of a collection. And all those monsters, boy, do they have some party.

He told me about his daughter. Miranda. His stories of her felt like me. That's how come I could get at him; I knew her so well. After he left I had to call, explain things. It's policy. Dumbfuck policy, but you know how policy gets. It's stick to it or your job.

It was just my luck she answered the phone.

"Hi," she said, all breathless, like I was her girlfriend or someone she'd been expecting.

I sat there in that grey walled room, phone in one hand, his gun in the other. I'd made him leave it, but now I was wishing I hadn't. I was thinking I would shoot myself instead of talk to her. Not for her, you understand. For me it would be easier. But I did. Tell her. I told her her daddy wasn't coming home any more. Told her why, what it was he'd planned. Told her things he'd said, things no one in the world but her could've known. Things that made her breathing go funny over the phone.

I hoped she wasn't crying. I wondered what it looked like, the room she was sitting in. Not grey. Please, for her sake, let it not be grey.

"I hate him," she said, when she could say something.

"I know, honey. I know. He won't hurt you now."

Now, if he hurts anyone, it'll be himself. But I didn't say that part, didn't tell her I couldn't get rid of the monster, could only turn it inside out.

"I only know your word that what you said he was gonna do is true. I know you said you made it so he's never coming back. I know I loved my daddy. I love him. Even right now I do."

His gun lay stupid in my lap, stupid and silent. I couldn't use it now. I never could have used it. On me. On anyone. I'm just not made that way. She'd led me to the spot, the one we come to, all of us, sooner or later. The spot that was my job. Take people there, take them out of it again. If you can. Everyone but me. For me the spot was made of memory, the feeling of a little girl I'd been, all crumpled up and thrown away. Was still. So I told her. I couldn't do anything else, just tell her and tell her, how it had been with me and him.

She listened to me, like the little trouper she was.

She was just a kid, like I'd been. Only for me there hadn't been anyone to explain. Why I survived, when my testimony sent my daddy away for good. That I loved him too, always would, no matter how much I hated him. That neither love nor hate would make me free.

That it was him who was bad, and not me.

And after I'd said goodbye to her his monster was still with me, sticky like glue. I felt like it was mine now, and not his. Even after four years, you sometimes forget how to let it go. His murderous heart was circling me, in orbit around my soul like a darkened moon.

"Where'd you get that?"

"Only one place this comes from," I said, smearing a line of blue powder down my nose. "Help yourself."

But he was already painting it around his eyes, laughing at himself, a blue raccoon. That's how it works. It sinks into the skin, gets absorbed into the bloodstream.

Finds the heart, the brain.

"Thank you for loving me as much as you do," said Little Davis.

Oh, the Blues, you learn to live the Blues. The Blues is what we call it because of its colour, little packets of blue powder, fringe benefits to the trade. If you have the habit you're Living the Blues. Officially it's not habit forming but what else could it be for how it makes you feel. Like you're loved. Like you love. Love. That's our other name for it.

Love and Blues, two opposite kind of names, for the paradox it is, the double edged blade. We're given an allotment to use in therapy on the clients where nothing else works; sometimes it can make people see the truth of themselves, but without violence, without pain. Makes them able to perform that open heart surgery of the psyche that is necessary to their survival, to ours. Gives them a little light to travel their dark river. We are only their guides, and not always good ones. We suffice.

Ostensibly the government bureaucrats who administer the Clinics issue it to us for therapeutic use only, but they give us a lot more than we need to patch up all the broken suckers that walk in the door. It's an open secret that it's our danger pay. The breakdowns, the burnouts among therapists are so high they know the only way they can keep us is with the Blues. And by the time we realize how dangerous, how hard the work really is, and are ready to quit, we're hooked. By then we're strung out. 'Cause after you've emptied yourself, after you've torn yourself into tiny pieces leading some poor stranger home, you need a little solace for yourself as well, a little Love to get you through the night. And after a while you just need.

It took Little to teach me that as good as it works, it isn't the real thing. You lose that distinction. If you ever knew the difference, you forget. Little died, and I remembered. It's an imitation, and a cheap one, and the closest so many people ever get to love.

"How much did it cost?"

"Did what cost?" asks Benji, rolling a joint.

"Your peace," I say. "I don't trust it. You got to tell me how much it cost." Benji. For the first time I see what looks like an emotion on her face. A little half smile like a voice breaking. Since Chuckie went away, Benji has learned how to be still, how to be alone. But some-where it still hurts. I can tell. In this business, you learn all the signs.

"It cost," says Benji. "It cost."

"You just like the wife killers, Benji." I say it through my teeth, slouching way down in the grey chair: "You just like the twisted fuck-ers you is paid to fix. You just ain't as far gone."

"How so?" asks Benji, supercilious, raising an eyebrow. In this business, we learn bad games. We even learn to like them.

"You just like them, Benji. Deep down all you want is to be loved."

She laughs. Benji's laugh. "And you, Ruby, what do you want?"

"That is so easy, Benji, so easy. I want Little to be alive again. I didn't love him enough. That's why he dead, Benji, because of me. His jalloo murdered him, but it could just as well have been me."

"But honey," she says, "you didn't even know what love was. How could you know, being what you are?"

We went home to my place. We walked there, stopping in alleyways to paint ourselves with blue graffiti. I live in a loft, further down the river on Kenya Road. All the way there Little kept telling me he loved me. It got to be embarrassing. This guy is such a kid, I'd think, letting the stuff go to his head so much.

"I love you, Ruby," he said. "I really love you."

We were lying on the Chinese rug, listening to music, staring at the ceiling. Painting it Blue.

"Yeah, honey, I know. I love you too." And I'd roll over to change the music, to reach for more. And I thought I did. He was so beautiful. His eyes like the ocean, washing through me. Telling me he loved me.

And I told him about Clinic. People love to hear that shit, why you work there, what it's really like. So you tell them, you give them some kicks. Cheap thrills for them, easy points for you. But with Little I somehow got it wrong. With Little I got it wrong right from the start.

"I don't want you to go crazy, Ruby," he said. "I love you too much." He was looking down at me, into my eyes. He was obstructing my view of the ceiling.

"What are you talking about, me going crazy?"

"All you people go crazy. I never met anyone before works River Street. I never thought I wanted to, heard you were all crazy. But you're not crazy at all, and now, I don't want you to be. You're different. You're not like I expected."

"Listen," I say, propping myself up on an elbow, "crazy is part of the job. Psychosis in a controlled environment. So it doesn't happen out on the street. But you got to go with them, to where they go. And keep one foot on the beach, so's you can lead them back out. Only sometimes you don't come back. Sometimes they pull you in and drown you. I've felt it happening. Benji got me out one time, cut me loose. Some of them you got to let them go. We're still human, we government workers. It's hard sometimes, to remember there's that one or two a year, you got to cut them loose. It becomes a point of pride, fixing people. But it's better to lose them than yourself as well. They put those ones on drugs, keep them locked up like they used to. There's not many anymore. Not nearly as many as there used to be. Because of us."

"But they don't pay you enough, Ruby. Even this," he says, stroking my arm, leaving blue trails there, "this is lovely, but it isn't enough."

"I love you too, baby."

And after that he just tried to make me laugh.

And he did. He made me laugh for weeks, while we stayed high. I didn't go in to work, except to pick up my ration of Blues. Because I'm good, Frankie put up with it. And because Benji told him I was in love. And every day Little made me feel younger.

I felt young again, and I felt evil. I kept turning my back on it, thought it was residue from my last jalloo I couldn't shake off. But it wouldn't rub off, wouldn't come off, no matter how much Blue I scrubbed at it with, how much Love. No matter how much of Little I used. But it was mine. It was my very own monster.

I didn't know that then. I didn't know it when we didn't have enough anymore to keep the two of us going and Little came home one day, telling me he'd filled out an application for a job at the Clinic. I didn't even suspect when I heard myself tell him how good he'd be. It's a No Experience Preferred type of gig. They train you; it's based on a personality profile they get from a bunch of tests they run on you. But I didn't need to see the test results; I knew they'd accept him. He'd be better than me, better than Benji even. He had the dotted line around him, could merge, join others; see with them.

The night before he was to start training we thought we'd celebrate, do up what we had left in one big bang. And when the sky outside turned the same colour with morning, Little told me he loved me again.

"I love you too, baby. I love you because you're so beautiful..."

Only this time, Little told me no.

"No," he said. "You don't love me. That's just the Blues talking, and now you've made me hear them too. They've fucked me up, and I'm hard to fuck. I got too much polish, most things just slide right off. But the Blues has stuck, has made me need what I thought was just a good time. Not like you. You I loved from the start, although you never would believe me. You tried to buy me, Ruby. Didn't think you were worth shit, didn't think I could love you for yourself."

I went to the bathroom and locked the door, looked at myself in the mirror. Listened to his footsteps follow me, stop outside. Listened how his voice had gone quiet. Scary quiet. Saying: "You don't love me. You think I'm just some dream the Blues dreamed up. You don't even know what love is."

I looked at myself in the mirror. Opened my mouth. Heard: "You never could handle your drugs. You're just a kid. Go to bed, get some sleep. We can talk about it in the morning, you still want. If you remember." Then I turned the shower on, loud, so I wouldn't hear what else he might have to say. So he wouldn't hear me crying.

He forgave me. To prove it he even moved his stuff into my place. He didn't have much. Some clothes. A photograph album of some family. I threw that out, jealous. The only pictures I still had of family were scratched onto my brain, no matter how hard I tried to get rid of them. But Little forgave me.

It was hard, always being forgiven. Before, he'd always made me laugh, but now he had me taking showers all the time. I was never cleaner.

He finished training, started his first case. Frankie started him on an easy one, a teenage girl who'd had her heart broke. But Little was good, too good; he didn't just heal her, he left her singing. And maybe that is what healing is, after all.

But it wasn't just the first one; it was all his jalloos that followed. They all came away clean as spoons. Little spent himself for all of them like he was a stock market crash about to happen. When it came to throwing pearls before swine, he was the prince. And I thought it was just he was new to the Blues.

He said it was the money he liked. He did, too, money he had for the first time. He bought presents for his friends, silk kimonos he had sent from Japan. For Benji, a turquoise one, with dragons embroidered in silver and gold.

For her to dance in. Little loved to watch Benji dance.

"When you dance," he told her, "I don't need much more in the world." And she danced more often, because of it.

Sometimes he gave money to strangers in the street. "I like to make people feel better," he'd say. It wasn't only the money. Little loved his work; he thought it mattered.

Living the Blues with you. We'd come off case and go dancing in the clubs that line the river: The Ocean, 1001 Knights, Kenya. Little knew all the doors and bartenders from his days as a performance artist; we never paid covers, and our first rounds always came on the house. They welcomed him home, his people. With me it was different; Little introduced me as his best friend, as the love of his life, but they turned away, mouths sharpening at the corners. I was the magician, the one who'd disappeared him, brought him back transformed: a therapist at River Street. The job attracts rumour mongering faster than illicit sex. I played mysterious woman for them. I know all the lines; for some jalloos, it's the only game in town, at least at the beginning. When the clubs emptied at four there'd be parties, speakeasies, restaurants. And then we'd go home. Every morning between jobs we'd see the sun come up from my big factory windows. We'd see the sky change colour, shift from black to violet to blue. Blue. Washes of Blue. Awash in Blue.

"It's good," he said. "You're very good."

"This is all I've ever wanted." And it was.

But the morning came that Little disappeared; lost me in the crowd of night faces, slipped away on the dance floor at Kenya.

I looked everywhere. I spent fortunes on a half-awake cabdriver, asking him to wait outside. He waited, and I always came out alone. He grumbled at me in his rear view mirror, telling me I'd never learn. Finally he drove me home.

No Little there to kiss me to sleep, just a hollow in my gut where he'd been. The bed was big and grubby; the morning light too critical for the dust we were always too happy to clean. I got dressed again and walked over to the Fifth Street Deli, and on my way there clouds came, and it started to rain. With the rain, even the pigeons took cover.

It was noon when he found me at my table, littered with newspapers, coffee cups, Kleenex. He ordered a tea and sat down across from me. He looked different; I was withered, shrunken, but the hours had changed Little the other way; he was more substantial. His body took up space, filled the room; I'd only seen him float before. But Little wasn't dancing anymore.

"You shouldn't have done that, Little."

"Ruby."

"How come you done what you did?"

"We're going to quit."

"Quit? What are we going to quit? You don't want me anymore. Is that what you're trying to say?"

"No. No, it's not, stupid. You and I are going to quit our jobs at River Street. Preferably we are going to quit this town, this country. We are going to quit."

"You sure know how to ruin a good thing, baby."

It seems he'd seen a friend turn blue. The other kind. From lack of breath. They are always cooking up new drugs to dump on the street, and this one hadn't passed the test. Or it had. Whichever way you look at it.

"Drugs are thieves," Benji always said.

"The Blues is just the same, Ruby. Maybe it don't steal your breath but it numbs your soul. Just because it's government run doesn't mean it's exempt. Especially because. I don't need to see it, what's happening to us. To you, especially. I'm new to this game, but you, Ruby, are going nowhere fast."

Big deal, I figure. I've been going nowhere fast my whole life and I still haven't arrived.

"Yeah sure, Little," I say. "We quit. You and me. You gonna go back to dancing on tables at The Ocean? That silver paint shit for your skin, Little. You know some other way to feel this good?"

"It doesn't look to me like you feel very good, Ruby." And then he looked tired. I'd never seen him look tired before. It made me feel sad to know even Little could get burned out. That he would get old. I put my hand over his.

"Come on," I said. "Let's go home."

We're sitting at the big factory windows, looking down at the ships. I've told you we'll quit, but I'm afraid. I'm afraid if I take away the Blues this will be gone too, these moments with you. Without the Blues, you'll see me as I really am, and, having seen, you'll leave me.

Why would you stay?

I remember what it was like here, before you came. I'd sit at this window for hours at a time, smoking cigarettes, watching the river. And towards dawn, when the loneliness got too sharp, when the memories of my father came crowding in, I'd reach for the Blues. I'd send him away again, send him drifting down the long blue river of forgetting. Then when he was gone, I'd be alone. And I would dance. And in the morning, there would be birds.

There's silence between us as we sit here, watching the river. Palpable silences I can touch, that I know will open, will draw apart like a curtain, giving birth to what?   Little hands me the joint, as though, holding it, I'll be defenceless, will have to listen. And he tells me I am proud to be a scar.

I don't say anything, because the curtains are drawing apart, and they're taking my breath with them. I can't speak, so Little tells me what I'm saying.

"It's like you say to everyone, "You can't hurt me, see how hurt I am already." You do yourself in so there's only leftovers for the rest of the hyenas. You take all their glory away—and you think that's good enough—you think you've won. But you ain't. 'Cause when you're Blue you're stuck, you never get to rise above it, to where the real colours are. The colourful colours. There's always been people who really do love you, Ruby. There always will be. You're lucky that way. For some people, there really isn't anyone. You've met enough of them on the job. You should be able to tell the difference."

He gets up, goes over to the stereo, turns the music down.

"You're right. Most people don't give a shit about you. But the ones who really do care, you should treat them well."

The curtains are all the way open now and I'm trying as hard as I can to feel what's there, what it is they've opened to. Because it can't be seen. You have to feel it.

And I think maybe it's love. The other kind I hadn't known existed. I think maybe this time I can finally afford to believe, that this time he's given me the currency I need to hear the words only love could make him speak. I wonder from who Little learned it. He's only twenty years old. I wonder who made Little get so wise.

He comes walking back towards me. He's wearing a red kimono. With birds of paradise. At least, I think that's what they are.

"Treat yourself well, Ruby. You, more than anyone, deserve it."

But I don't. I don't deserve it. I don't deserve him. If I had, I wouldn't have tried to buy him. For a moment you get a glimpse of it, your chance at happiness, but it's not a real chance, because no one gets happiness, at least I've never met anyone who did. It's just a trick, to let you know what you're missing. So that it hurts more, when you wake up, and things are the same as they ever were.

"You're too smart," I say. "You're too good-looking. You make me feel old, and I'm only twenty-six. And you make me feel ugly, and dumb. You're too fucking good. You're too perfect. Let up a little, will ya? Give the rest of us gimps a chance."

He looks at me from so far away, as though the room just grew a million miles long. I can't make out his face and I don't know if it's because I'm crying or because he is.

"Go away," I say. "The Blues has scrambled your brains, baby. Leave me alone."

He goes. From far away across the room I watch him go, walk ever so slowly towards the bedroom door. I sit where I am, frozen to death. I want to call him back but I don't know how. I've never done it before. At the door he stops, turns.

"I don't believe you," he says. "I can't believe you are really such an asshole, Ruby. A real live honest-to-god asshole."

"You just a kid," I say, from where I'm sitting, frozen. The words come out of my mouth like they're someone else's, but I can't stop them, I can't help what they say.

And because, after all he is just a kid who loves me, he goes.

And in the morning he gets up and goes to work on a case he never comes back from.

Benji is gone now, and I am alone in this room. This room, made, like any other room, of walls. Grey and carpeted, soft to mute the sounds that fear makes.

Before she left, Benji told me about her case, a man who said he'd come for sex. Somewhere he'd heard that's what we were. People hear things. It took her a long time to bring him round to seeing what his real problem was. Himself. As usual. You get so tired.

Hookers. We had a big laugh over that one, me and Benji. It's our souls we measure out here, one little piece at a time. Some nights I think I'd rather be out on the street, out there in the traffic, with the red taillights.

We are inside, always inside, enclosed by soft grey walls of fear.

"I want to possess you," he kept telling her. A real jalloo. Benji laughed, imitating him. She left me, went back to finish him off, still laughing. Maybe it was always the same, but tonight her laugh seems colder, tonight it freezes me so solid I feel I'm made not of ice, but of stone.

Possession. Only death possesses you now, Little, neither I nor the man who wanted too much of you. I never meant to get this old, not with these eyes. I'm just a kid, really; it was easy to be tough when I had you to laugh with. Used to be your thin arms would encircle me from behind and my skin would be alive again, just for a moment, before I went to sleep. Like it wasn't for anyone else. Since Marianne.

Why do people want to buy sex? Sex is so easy to come by.

If I could, I would buy love.

If it were for sale.

No matter how much it cost.

I have seen the ugliest eyes. You get rubbed to raw in this place, ugliness rubbing itself up against you like sandpaper, jealous that you still hope. You get a habit to put up between you and them, you buy yourself designer eyes, fashionable and cold, empty as hell.

You was the best of all of us, Little. They couldn't shovel in the money or the Blues fast enough for what you gave them. And they knew it. It made them proud, the ugly ones.

The ugly ones. It took an ugly one to know what I couldn't, what you were worth. Made him so jealous he had to snap out that light if he couldn't make it his own. But it could never be owned, that light. Not by him, not by me. Not by the Blues.

Sentiment. When the feeling's gone, you replace it with sentiment. Cheap sentiment and superstition. No matter how many times you told me.

I really love you, Ruby, I really do.

And I survive. Used to wish I could die, used to wish I could get dead. Used to think I'd never live this long, not in this business. But since I've learned that you hang on, you hang on, dead as you might wish to get. I do not live so sharply any more. My edges are worn and so I bounce, I don't clatter now, I don't shatter.

I remember one time me and you rode the bus together, going home to my place after we'd been out dancing all night. It was so late they were going to work already, the nine to fivers, and we started kissing, just to jack them up. It was easy to make them jealous of us, because we looked so happy; we were young and good looking and we made each other crazy.

I remember I used to mix my own colours of nail polish in those days and I used to try and get it to match your turquoise eyes. So we were sitting on this bus kissing and my hand was resting on your cheek and I took my tongue out of your mouth and pulled my face back just enough so I could see how well I'd matched it...and I had, exactly, until we got off the bus, because under the sky your eyes looked like they were lit from the inside, and they haven't invented the nail polish yet that can do that...

...I used to love to dress up with you and go out on the street and be stared at...it made me feel like a queen from another planet...

Now I think I'd like to be on an airplane with you. On the way to Japan, to a place like Kyoto: a raked garden, full of stillness.

Mostly I want not to be broken any more, to no longer be afraid of winter because it makes everything come apart; I want to pull myself back towards the sun from this place where I am now, wherever it is, it's scary.

I've sent along this story as Candas chose it for Prairie Fire Vol. 15, No. 2. It was the Summer 1994 issue, and appeared in conjunction with ConAdian, the 52nd Worldcon in Winnipeg.It's not the only story of mine she's chosen for an anthology, but it's the one I like today.

I haven't touched it except to exchange telephone for phone. Maybe telephone could have stayed, if the world in "One Day" is an alternate reality and not the future. Could be. But telephone jumps out, and phone gives us legroom. I also added the name of the Zen garden in Kyoto, Ryōan-ji, which I have since been to see, on a visit to Japan with family in 2011.

It wasn't quiet at all, but teeming with crowds.

THE SECRET OF FREEDOM

The shadows of the Forest of Thorns shift and twist as we creep between the spindly branches that reach out to reach out to block the path. Kerr is focused on the ground in front of us, searching for the tracks of the beast that's been attacking the outbuildings. If he notices the way the forest marks our movements, he doesn't show any sign of it, so I do my best to do the same.

"Bear, I think," he whispers, studying the clearest track we've found. The paw print is as large as his hand, sunk deep into the soft earth of the forest floor.

"Starving?"

"Berserk." He points to the rim of the print, the red glow that resembles embers, but carries not even a whisper of fire song. Kerr rises from his crouch and steps over a low-hanging branch as he follows the passage of the bear. The forest should have broken branches and slashed trees to match the broken doors and damaged walls of our outbuildings, but this forest protects itself, which is, of course, how it protects us. I watch the shadows reach for Kerr and shiver. Sometimes, it doesn't seem that protection is worth the cost.

My grandmother said the forest didn't exist when she was young. She said the keep was protected only by its placement in the cliffs and the sealed gate and the outbuildings were left to fend for themselves during inevitable raids. Năinai's home had been burned to the ground three times before the plant charmer was born and bound. With his power the Chief raised the forest around Kitamaat, providing shelter and an extra layer of defense to them all. Despite the failures of our past, the Chiefs have never learned that all magic comes with a price. When she'd first told me that, I'd wondered what price I had paid for the gift I kept hidden. Wondered what price Jun had paid, though I learned the answer to that soon enough.

I glanced over my shoulder, peering into the darkness behind us, even though I knew the entrance to the forest was long out of sight. Jun was there behind us, maybe even waiting at the edge. There's magic in the forest that kept him from entering as surely as it kept out our enemies and there was no way to ask Kerr to grant him passage without revealing his existence and inviting dangerous questions.

"You cannot speak to him, child," Grandmother had whispered, her hand brushing my hair as I cried over the teasing of the other children. "Not when there is anyone to hear."

"Not even mother and father."

"Most especially not them."

"It's not fair."

"Very little is, child, not here, not for you."

I hadn't understood it, then. There were no magic users in the tribe, then, at least none whose abilities had been discovered. There was no telling how many might be hiding, as I was, afraid of the consequences. It wasn't until Brier was revealed, her power placed under the control of the Chief through the leather bindings strapped to her wrist that I grasped the danger. Brier weaves illusions with more skill than I have at fire song, but now if she does so for herself, the bindings punish her. Her greatest talent and she can only use it by order of the Chief, or his kin.

Kerr stops short, raising his hand. I hold my breath as I wait, watching him inch forward, moving branches out of his way. "This can't be." He steps slowly through the parted branches, letting them fall back to fill the space of his passage. I hesitate, biting my lip, and then shuffle through. There is space on the other side, like a clearing, in a forest where none should exist. "It looks like a road."

"It was used as one," he says, studying the ground. "Not enough for an entire army, but there's at least two wagons. How did they get through?"

The edges of the forest glimmer. It reminds me of the berserker's trail and, though it's lower than a whisper, I can hear the fire song if I listen. The song is chaotic, as all fire song is, but directed, controlled. "They used a fire singer." I follow the dying notes until I find a patch of grass still struggling to burn. If I want, I can pick up the traces of the song, help the struggling flames regain their strength and make more roads in our forest. Was this why the Chiefs kept us bound? Paranoia keeping them from trusting even the magic users who were the source of our protection. It was as good an excuse as any for something that could not be excused. "Magic enough to counter ours."

Kerr joins me and watches as the flames finally lose the battle against the forest's regeneration. Without the singer's lure and encouragement, the fire isn't strong enough to take hold. "The road will close soon, but if they've come this far, they may have reached the keep. We have to go back." When he runs, I follow chasing the raiding party set for our home.

I can only hope my brother can keep them from burning a path through our village as they have burned a path through our forest. See them, Jun, I think, though I've never had reason to believe he can hear me. See them and protect the keep. The army will take care of the raiding party, but the fire singer is another matter altogether.

Is it worse, I wonder, to have to keep silent when only one person can hear you, or to be able to talk when no one can? It's a question I've pondered on and off my entire existence, but I've never reached a satisfactory answer. When Li is here, she has such a hard time pretending I'm not. If I make a joke she'll laugh, if I make a comment, she'll sometimes answer. It's too risky. So I spend a lot of my time not saying anything at all. If she were discovered, if they put those bindings on her wrists because of me, I'd never be able to forgive myself. Better to just hold all my thoughts inside.

When she's not here, though, I can say what I want. What is the point, though, in talking to people who will never hear you?

Not that Anna could hear me even if I were alive to speak. She's hammering away at a new sword, forcing the metal into the shape demanded by the Chief, though he has swords enough for his army three times over. Mother used to say it was good work, necessary work, when our father worried, but she had the same exhaustion in every strike that her former apprentice is showing now. Anna's newest order, the one taken away with the raiding party this morning, was almost too much and now the Chief has demanded another of the same size. But Anna is still here working, not taken away to travel with the army as our mother had been, leaving her shop to her apprentice, who kept it going when mother did not return.

"We don't need this many swords," I say as she stills the hammer and turns the glowing metal to the waiting bucket. Though sometimes I think it would be better to let the metal shatter, to ruin the shape, I sing the water to even temperature and coverage, to exactly what it needs for the best blade to form strong and true. No one will ever use it, our army is not that big, but it will be perfect, just as demanded.

A shiver runs up my back, an unusual and unexpected sensation, as I have no nerves to respond to sudden changes. I turn toward the window, see Brier creeping by though I could have sworn I saw her with the raiding party this morning and the Chief would not have left her power behind. I leave Anna stripping off her heavy apron and step out of the smithing hut. There is smoke rising from the forest of thorns, thick grey plumes that rise above the canopy and reach to the clouds drifting above.

"The forest is on fire."

No one can hear me. I spin back to the hut where Anna is resting before the starting the next sword. The water bucket sits, stable and secure beside her station, the water placid and content. I call to it, disturb its contentment, rise up its spirit and let it strain against the barrier of the bucket. Water does not, by nature, move on its own, but it stirs when called by wind or magic and my song urges it roll the bucket to the door as it spills forth to its freedom.

Anna cries out in surprise and confusion, and follows the bucket to the door. She bends to pick it up and when she rises, she sees the forest and the smoke. Her face goes slack in shock, but then she does what I cannot and raises the alarm. People pour from the outbuildings, flowing like a rushing river toward the keep and its promise of safety. I flow against them, in the opposite direction, but no one notices. Perhaps there are some benefits to not having a physical form.

By the time I reach the edge of the forest I can hear the song beneath the static of the shades. Someone is calling to the fire. Not Li, though she's the only fire singer who should be anywhere near, but another voice, deeper, more practiced. Trained.

The clouds still float above the rising smoke, fat and happy in a day that's perfect for carrying them about. Reaching them is more difficult than reaching the bucket, but I do not have to worry about anyone hearing me scream. I call to the clouds to bring forth the rain.

The sky darkens as the clouds pull more water into them, as they grow restless and unsettled. The song stirs their discomfort until the water grows too heavy to float in the sky and drops upon the Earth below, falling on the keep, the outbuildings, and the forest. There's a hesitation in the fire song growing ever closer, but the singer recovers. They give the fire strength it would not have otherwise, the strength to consume the thorns and the strength to withstand the rain.

I've never had to sing a dual song before. Calling to the clouds, dropping the rain, takes one measure. The rain falling and withstanding the fire takes another. If I leave one too long, the rain lessens or the fire grows. I cannot do this alone. I need Li.

Rain, there is rain. I breathe a silent thanks to my brother as the water falls down on the scar left by the fire singer's passage. It might even be enough to keep them from the keep. It's a skookum storm, after all. Surely the singer cannot keep the fire going through so much? But then, they kept it going through the forest, against the efforts of the shades who are already beginning to recover the cleared ground. Charcoal is disappearing under fresh green, emboldened by the water. In less than a day, perhaps no more than a few hours, the exterior edges will be regrown and our defense secured again.

But the fire still burns. I can hear it now that we're out of the forest, a celebration as the outbuildings are consumed, as our homes are disappearing. It's joyous, controlled chaos, and I want to scream it silent.

"They saw," Kerr says, bending over to catch his breath, pointing to the outbuildings. Whoever is attacking has already passed beyond our sight, a mass of shapes gathering at the keep entrance barely visible through the rain. It is only those shapes, however, none of our people. "They've dropped the gate."

There's a flicker at the edge of my vision. The rain begins to ease as Jun says, "They've brought the fire with them. I can't stop it on my own."

I bite my lip to keep from responding, to keep the panic from my eyes.

"We have to get closer," Kerr says, "but be careful."

I nod and follow him as we leave the burnt path and slip through the smaller spaces between the buildings. We know them all, having grown up here. This is our home, our land, and it is on fire.

"Li, you have to do something."

If I sing, I'll be overheard. There's no chance that would go unnoticed. Jun knows this, he has to. Why is he asking it of me?

"Damn it," Kerr says, peering around the corner of what was once my mother's smithy. "The wall is on fire."

"The rain will put it out," I say and Jun swears.

"I'll do what I can," he says. Another flicker and he's gone, away from my side to who knows where. Maybe closer to the clouds that dump water on our heads in what seems like rivers. Still, beneath the downpour, the fire song burns. I've never heard another singer, aside from my brother. There's a discordance in what should be harmony, something that tells me it is not from here, not one of ours. Even as the fire bends and moves to answer, I can feel the strain, the extra effort it takes that I have never felt myself. This is our home. My home. These are our people and the flames, even stirred by an enemy, are ours.

There's another flicker at the corner of my eye and I freeze, expecting Jun and another lecture even as the rain continues to fall. It's not him, however.

"Brier," Kerr says, "what are you doing here?"

She slumps against the wall, her pale skin almost gray. Though her flowing sleeves cover her wrists, I can picture the bindings around them, the ones I fear being placed around my own.

"I was coming to find you," Brier said, "when the alarm was raised."

"You couldn't stop them?"

Her jaw clenches, but her voice is flat when she answers. "I need an order."

"Why didn't my father or sister issue one?"

"You don't know?"

"What have they done now?" It's not quite despair in the question, but close.

"They've taken the army to attack Seven Sisters."

"Damn it."

"Kerr, it's worse." She hesitates, just a moment before continuing. "They took every warrior we have. We've got only a handful of guards left. If they take down the gate, we're lost."

Kerr slumps against the wall, staring at the bow in his hand. He's good, we all know it, one of the best the clan has ever seen, but what is one bow against an entire army? "If you got an order, what could you do?"

"My best," she says, "but they've got a singer. I can't stop the fire. They'll hear it, no matter what I make them see."

"Do everything you can to protect the keep," he says, though the order doesn't sound comfortable coming off his lips.

Brier nods and disappears again. At least using her powers now won't cause her so much pain. She can save us. She can turn it around.

"Li," Kerr says, "you need to take a message to the Chief."

"I haven--"

"There's no time for ceremony. All the other messengers are inside." He grasps my shoulder. "I grant you passage through the forest. Tell my father what has happened here."

"Yes, sir."

Orders given, he runs from building to building, creeping closer to the keep that still burns. Closer to where our whole clan waits, hiding from the flames.

Clouds, once encouraged, let everything go. Unlike the water in the bucket, they'll continue until there's nothing left to give. I let the song take on its own life and watch the army below. The walls of the keep are a cliff face, the ground forced up and out when the Awakening split the world and the let the other side fall into the ocean. It's too far away, too far below, to be of any use to us now, the rolling song almost taunting.

On the other side, where the attackers gather, there is fire like an ocean growing in defiance of the rain. I can pull enough to drench it on one side, but by the time I move across it's grown to fill in the places left behind and I cannot keep the water flowing against its nature long enough to smother it all. From here I cannot see the fire singer, can't even really see the army, the fire blocks it all. It blocks our archers as well, though they're firing arrows through the flames in the hopes of hitting something, anything, at all. It isn't going to work. For the first time in our history, someone is going to be able to take down the door.

I return to Li, only to find her running back to the forest. "Where are you going?"

"I'm to take a message to the Chief, to bring the army back."

"There isn't enough time."

"It's what I was told to do."

"Li, stop, you can't do this." I move to block her.

She hesitates and then charges forward, right through me.

It's like being pulled apart, thread by thread, my existence a tapestry shredded by a careless child. Then she's through and it all pulls taunt, back into place in the way living things never can. "Li!"

"Come with me," she says, still backing toward the forest.

"I can't."

"There's a road! Until the forest takes it back, there's a path through. It let the raiding party in, it can let you out. If we hurry, we can be gone before the forest takes it back."

She's really leaving, telling me to leave. Can she not see? "They'll be dead by the time you deliver your message, all of them."

She stops. "What are you talking about? The gate..."

"They're breaking it down as we speak."

"The guards will pick them off before then."

"Not with the fire there, especially not when the rain is needed to keep it from getting worse. They can't see their targets, Li. There's nothing they can do. If you leave now, there will be nothing left for the army to save."

"But if I stop it..."

"I know it's a risk." Though we're far away, I know there is a part of her still listening to the song of the flames, drawn to it, wanting to stir it up and hear its joy. It's more difficult for her already, having to do so when no one can hear her or discern what she's doing. "You might not be able to sing for yourself again."

"It's not just that." Her words are spaced out, slow and considered, though we have no time for this.

It's a change of positions that doesn't suit us. It should be her in a hurry, alive and vibrate as the flames, and me with all the time in the world, like a river creating a gorge. "Then what is it?"

She stares at me, as if I should already know the answer. "Why can't you enter the forest?"

"Why can--" The song of the rain isn't tiring yet, but it's beginning to dwindle. There is only so much water in the sky and I've never tried to coax it back up to fall again. If she keeps delaying, I may have to see if that's possible. "What has that got to do with anything?"

"Something keeps you out, the same thing that keeps other magic out."

I still don't see her point.

"Jun, if they bind me, what if I won't be able to see or hear you anymore?"

If I had breath, I expect I'd be holding it now. I've never even considered that, but I suppose it's possible. We do not know what it is that ties us to one another, after all, except that we are fire and water together. In that way, I suppose, it makes sense to think whatever it is that keeps her from her own power would keep her from me.

"You'll be alone. We both will, but you..."

She doesn't finish, but I do. "No one will ever know I'm here." There are so many people in that keep right now, who don't know that I exist. The only one I've ever had in the world was Li. All the same, they are our tribe, mine as much as hers. "We can't let them die just on the chance that might happen."

"Jun, please, I can't." Her body is trembling and I don't think it's from the cold of the rain. "Please, let me leave."

"What will you do once you reach them? Let them lead you back to the burnt out husk? March until he sends you into battle to die like our parents?"

"Once I've delivered the message, I'll be on the other side of the forest. I'll be able to get away."

"You're going to run."

"It's always been the plan."

"That was before death reached our door."

"It was always going to come at some point. We knew that. Leaving them has always meant leaving them to our enemies in some fashion."

"But not when you could have made a difference. Can you really live free knowing you didn't even try?"

From the direction of the keep there's a loud crash, wood on wood. A battering ram, no doubt. "I have to keep the gate soaked. It'll go down faster if the fire gets to it." I leave without turning to look at her again. If she runs, I don't want to see it.

~*~

Năinai once said the Forest of Thorns was our protection and our prison. It keeps attackers out, usually, but it keeps us in unless the Chiefs bid us leave. All I've wanted my entire life is that permission, permission I now have, but at what cost? The keep is a shadow in the rain, the fire nothing more than a glow and a song. It's easy, now, to pretend none of this is happening, none of this is real. It's easy to pretend it will all still be standing when I get back, but the storm has intensified over the gate and I know Jun was right. If I go now, there will be nothing for the Chief to save.

Shades are whispering in the forest behind me, reminding me it's there, reminding me I could go now, be away forever. Instead, I run to the heart of the rain, following the defiant fire song at the door of our home. I hide again at the edge of the blacksmith's hut. The forge is still humming, the fire not doused as it should have been. It must have happened quickly. Anna's in the keep, then, somewhere on the other side of the door, possibly even conscripted onto the wall to try and mount a defense. Like our mother who trained her, she'll be called into service to defend the tribe, even at the cost of her life. It costs us each something.

Jun was right about the fire. It burns at the base of the door and up along the walls, bright enough to create a blind under which to hide. At first, I think it's only the song that keeps it so, but then I see the attackers are feeding it, using poles to raise oil-soaked rags above their heads. It's only the song keeps the flames from eating away at the poles, from following the oil down onto the attacking army. They should have been more careful.

It would be difficult, perhaps impossible, to counter the song that prevents the fire from going out, as I'm untrained and the other singer clearly isn't. I don't have to do that, though. I just have to coax the fire in the other direction.

With a last whispered plea of remaining undiscovered, I begin to sing. The flames react, as they always have, my voice given edge by the recognition of my home. I use it to coax the flames down from their perch, to spread from the wrapped rags to the slick poles, leading it down to where their fuel has dripped onto the ground among the attackers.

They do not notice, not at first. There isn't even a change in the song. When the flames catch one of their uniforms however, someone shouts.

"Kendrick! Keep it under control!"

The song changes, calling the fire back up the poles, but as it does, the flames against the gates weaken. Hope jumps in my chest as I realize the singer must split his attention. He must work against both myself and my brother, either keeping the fire alive or keeping it where they need it. Better trained he may be, but this could give us the advantage. I return my focus to the flames, luring them down with the promise of the uniforms and the raiding supplies they've brought.

"Fuck, Kendrick, what are you doing?"

His song stops completely and the fire races to the waiting army, seeking out the temptations I have promised.

"They've got a singer," a voice hoarse from use says. "Find her."

I creep around the edge of the building as some of the attackers begin the hunt. They'll find me, they'll hear me, but I do not need to see the gate to keep the song going. Now that I know what they've brought to my home, I know how to keep the fire moving. As the warriors draw closer, I run. The maze of the out buildings give me the advantage, the narrows I have played in since I was a child, chasing my unseen brother in a game of hide and seek no one else could ever join.

The rain lets up before they catch me, the other fire singer's song quiet. I keep mine going, keep it chasing the army, though I no longer have the rain to help hide me. Instead, I turn back to the keep gate again, back to where the fire has taken over oil and tunic and in some cases started on flesh. I don't encourage that, but I do not stop it. They are still a threat, though the singer is quiet. When I reach the keep I run through the flames, keeping them from touching me, but granting a barrier. It's as effective for me as it was for them.

I press my back against the still-wet wood of the gate, strong and secure, and lead the fire to their battering ram.

"Stop her!" the fire singer croaks.

My vocal chords ache in unwilling sympathy, but I do not stop and they do not find me.

"The archers still can't see." Jun appears at my side. "Can you bring the flames down?"

They're wild, now, with more fuel than should be available, but fortunately, most of it is damp. I let go of the song, let the flames sputter where they can no longer hold purchase, going quiet as they go out. As they do, the arrows begin to fall. The guards are marksmen, straight and true, and the attackers scatter, someone sounding the retreat.

A large man slams into the wall next to me, eyes furious, an arrow in his shoulder. "You," he wheezes.

I back away from the angry fire singer and grab an abandoned sword. He is better trained in the song than I am, but I expect my rudimentary weapons training will be enough. I've never been taught to rely on my gifts, after all, the one benefit to having to keep it hidden.

As it happens, however, he is now alone, where I am not. A loud roar bellows from beside me and the shape of a brown bear corrupted with searing red stalks towards us. It lumbers, its movements reflecting the pain of its affliction and its mad eyes fixed on the fire singer. He turns from me to try and call to the flames, but the puddles have lapped themselves up and over everything that remains. There aren't even embers to answer him.

The bear roars again, charging, but before it reaches him an arrow strikes his throat, fired through the length of the bear. As the fire singer falls, the bear disappears in a shower of sparkles.

"Brier!"

The illusionist steps from between the buildings, her shirt soaked, long sleeves hanging from her wrists, the dark leather of the binding visible through the translucent fabric. Kerr follows behind her, a new arrow in his bow as he watches the singer for movement.

"He's not a warrior."

"He called the fire," I say, lowering my sword as they approach.

"You didn't go for the army," Kerr says, tucking the arrow back in his quiver.

"I thought I might be able to help."

"One sword against a whole raiding party?" he asks. It isn't censure in his tone, or even curiosity. It seems, if anything, he's giving me an opening.

I do not take it. "I thought the three of us might have a chance, with the rain."

Out of the corner of my eye, I can see Jun's smirk.

Kerr studies me for a moment and then nods. "It seems we did. I need to go inside and find out the damage. Then we need to see if another raid is coming. They cannot possibly have sent one so small to take down the entire keep. It wouldn't have been enough, if the army were here. I may need you to carry a message yet."

I bow as he leaves, a reflexive action, but perhaps not one he sees.

Brier wrings out the ends of her sleeves. "You were not relying on any sword," she says.

My gaze flickers to the bindings, still visible, always present.

"Don't worry." She flicks her sleeves loose again and for a moment I cannot see the source of her pain. "I won't tell anyone. After all, we should stick together here. Shouldn't we?" She offers me her hand.

"Don't trust her," Jun whispers.

I want to listen to him, but what choice do I have? We've taken the risk and now the results are as uncontrollable as the fire. I can only try to guide it. I take her hand and shake it. "So we should."

The Secret of Freedom is a story pulled from one work-shopped in a class of Candas' some years back. I've always thought some of the best teachers are the ones who can take things you thought you knew and get you to look at them from another angle. Candas is one of those teachers, so it's not surprising one of the lesson from her that

will always stay with me was a perspective change on word choice. I'd always looked at how it helps communicate character, action, and mood. However, it didn't occur to me, at least not in this way, how the words and names you chose could work against your world-building if they didn't make sense within the setting or world created. Also, by extension, how using specific words could reinforce those settings, especially when the world created is ours, but changed.

Candas taught me to think about the levels beneath the narrative, the ones that we carry with us by virtue of carrying the history of our language itself. It's a skill I expect I will eternally practice and never master, but I will always enjoy the challenge is presents.

AVOIDANCE

OK, I've screwed around long enough. I was given this writing assignment days ago, and haven't touched it until now. And I made sure
I kept busy until there was absolutely nothing left for me to do but
write a two hundred and fifty word sentence.

When I started cleaning my house, I vacuumed everywhere, trapping
dog and cat fur like small mice in the hose until all the floors were
bright and shiny and I could almost breathe again because I have al-
lergies, which I found out about when I joined a group, a women's
group, to find my purpose in life and have a reason for getting out of
bed every morning because it was getting harder and harder to do that,
and one of the first things we were all supposed to do in the group was
get an allergy test, but it wasn't the first thing I did, not by a long shot,
because I'd been dithering around at my life forever, acting as though
everything was great, fantastic, and actually my life wasn't bad, it was
just that sometimes I couldn't breathe, you know, but I finally did one
of the things we were supposed to do in order to truly begin to understand where our bodies were coming from, which was getting that
allergy test, and the really funny thing was that I already knew what I
was allergic to before I went in but it was like I couldn't trust myself
to know myself with any accuracy at all, and I wondered if it was be-

cause of the big lie I'd told myself for so many years, which was that everything was all right, that not being able to breathe was normal, and that I didn't have to understand where I was coming from. I just had to live with it.

I'm allergic to cats.

Once I finished the vacuuming, I washed and waxed the floors, and then washed and dried and folded and put away the laundry—including the sheets and blankets from every bed—before I cleaned the bathroom and then started on the windows, but the windows were a mistake and I made a hell of mess there, because it was nearly 20 below outside, and this place we bought didn't have windows that kept the cold out very well at all and I think I knew I was going to have trouble before I started but I kept going because I knew how long it had been since they had last been done, and I could feel this assignment hanging like an anchor around my neck even though I'd asked for it, begged for it really, because it felt like one of the best ways to get going again, and it had been so long since I'd written with any clarity and focus, and I missed it, I really did, but layered over that was the fear that I'd finally gotten to that age where there's nothing left for me to tell, which would have been the saddest thing in the world since I'd barely told any stories at all, and all my life I'd longed for the chance to do just that, but it felt like there were roadblocks every step of the way, and the thing I was most afraid of was finding out that I put those roadblocks up myself, just to make sure that I would never succeed.

I'm going to have to chip the ice off the windows.

After I finished cleaning and the house was as bright and shiny as I could make it, I almost stepped into my office to begin the assignment, but the dog was muling around my feet looking extremely sad, so I thought, "What the heck, I'll take him for a walk, just for a few minutes," and he was so happy when I grabbed my coat and mitts and didn't say "Go lay down Bear," like I say so often to him when I'm running off to another meeting or conference or presentation, just grabbed the leash and attached it to his collar and headed for the door, that I thought for a moment that he was going to jump right over me because sometimes, when that dog is extremely joyful, he can jump so high he looks over my head even though he's just a medium sized dog, or what I'd call more of an underachievement in the growing department even though we thought he was going to be as big as a Lab when my husband brought him—a cute little black bundle of fur that we all fell in love with—home, but he stopped growing at medium and kind of skinny, which is a nothing much kind of a dog, but he has a good heart, and I'm the one who walks him, and it's nice to have that reaction from someone when you do something for them, even though it was twenty below outside, and I knew we were both going to freeze our asses off.

He lasted a block and a half.

Once I'd thawed the ice from the dog's feet so he'd quit whining, I got supper on for the family, and since everyone had things to do that night I threw together a simple meal of soup and sandwiches, but I made the soup from scratch because my daughter had cooked a roast a few days before and I wanted to make certain that I used it all up before the roar that is work started for me again, and that I'd done something for my family before the roar that is work takes over my life again, because it always seems to take over my life no matter how hard I try to keep it in its place, and, after all, who doesn't like beef and barley soup, especially since I'd used a recipe I'd found in my grandmother's recipe book, which had been a gift from her just before she died, and when the soup was cooked and eaten and cleaned up— just the savoury smell hanging in the air like lingering ghosts of lives past—and I had wiped down the counters one last time before waving good-bye to my daughter as she headed off for work and kissing my husband good-bye as he headed off for a boy's night out, I had to admit that there was not another thing that stood in my way of beginning my writing again for real this time, with none of the hesitation that seems to be built into my system, and with none of the fear which goes hand in hand with the hesitation.

So, I wrote this.

I know that this anthology is supposed to be about Candas Jane Dorsey inspired science fiction, but I don't write that. (The closest I ever came to writing science fiction that was published was a short story about a vampire. Seriously.) But Candas has inspired me so much in my writing career that I finally decided this would be my entry. Not a science fiction story, but an essay about writing.

The first time I read it aloud was at the Women's Words Writing Week, put on by the University of Alberta's Women's Resource Centre and the Faculty of Extension, quite a few years ago. Candas Jane Dorsey ran the workshop I took, and even though I hadn't written the essay for the workshop, she convinced me that I should read it.

I did, and it was well received. That gave me the courage to believe that maybe, just maybe, I had what it took to be a writer. In fact, all of Candas's advice in that workshop—and in the years since—has helped me immensely in my writing journey, and I will be forever grateful to her for that.

But I'm still fighting the avoidance thing. I probably always will.

FATHER TIME

The bar I'm in is quiet. Three in the afternoon, not many people here. Two young men play darts against the far wall, and a middle-aged couple sit at a table with drinks. She smokes, he doesn't.

My waitress smiles sympathetically at me, knowing instinctively that something is wrong, but not sure what it is. I try to muster up a grin for her, but by the look on her face I'd say I've only managed to frighten her. She leaves my gin and orange on the table and walks away quickly.

I nurse the drink for a while, thinking about as little as I can manage. Too much thinking drags my mind back to the hospital; not a place I want it to be right now.

When my drink is about half-empty the outside door swings open and someone walks in, silhouetted against the bright sunlight. I squint for a moment, then turn my face away from the door.

So I hear, rather than see, the man come up to my table. I turn to tell him that I am not interested in company right now, but what I see stops me short.

The man, I realize, is my father. I am startled and it must show on my face. He smiles, and there are none of the lines that I know so well, the lines that have invaded his face with age.

I know this for a fact. I watched him as I grew, watched as he fought the losing Battle of Vanity. As the face that had once seemed so effortlessly smooth, so wonderful as a child in awe to stroke in wonder, slowly gave ground to the rifts and valleys of living.

This is my father as he was when he was a young man. But I just came from visiting my father in the hospital, where he is now losing an even more important battle.

The man who was my father steps up to me, and I reach out to stroke his face.

He lets me touch his skin for a second, and then says, "Let's go somewhere else and talk."

"This is my fifth trip," he says, after taking a sip of coffee. We are in The Silk Hat, in a booth near the back. He used to come in here and have his tea leaves read, but not today. What would tea leaves say about a man whose only reason for existence is an apparent quirk in the mathematics of the universe?

I watch the waitress as she goes by, uncomfortable talking while others are nearby. She goes to the only other occupied booth, near the door. We are near the back of the restaurant.

"Where do you go next?" I ask. It is hard for me to accept this, although not for the reasons you might think. Rather than being freaked by his being here, I am most bothered by the fact that he is appearing here younger than me.

"Ten more years. Each step takes me further away, but it seems to get easier."

"How..." I begin.

"Do I do it?" He shakes his head. "I can't explain. Even if I could, it would sound like a lot of spiritual mumbo-jumbo to you. What do people now call it? Sort of new age."

"Oh. You mean like mantras and crystals and stuff?"

"No." That's all he says.

I decide to change topics, although I realize as I speak I could have done better. "You realize you're dying."

He grimaces, and I see the first hints of those lines. "With?"

"Cancer. All through the body. Probably only days left." Tears start, I grab a napkin and try to staunch the flow.

He takes my hand and grieves with me. For himself.

I grieve for lost time.

The next day, he dies. I am downstairs having a cup of tea and thinking about when I was a child, and I feel a hand on my shoulder. It is the nurse; she has tears in her eyes. My father has been very popular here.

I stand too suddenly, knocking the cup to the floor. The tea that is left spills in slow-motion, and when it hits the floor it spreads in every direction. I feel the eyes of many people on my back right now, but those looks, whether judgemental or sympathetic, only touch me for the shortest of moments.

The nurse hugs me, briefly, then leads me to the elevator like I'm a little boy. Which is what I am right now, remembering stroking the smooth skin only yesterday, and then seeing the parched and sagging folds of his face today.

It was too much, and I had to leave. So I missed the moment of his death. We get off the elevator and the nurse takes me to the room and then leaves, shutting the door behind her.

His fault; he could have come to me after he died. As I look at the body one last time I punch the wall in fury and slide sobbing to the floor.

"I missed it," says a voice.

I look up, and there is my father. Only older than yesterday, by about ten years.

I don't talk to him, but rather I fold my arms and sulk. He's abandoned me, I hate him.

"I need your help. Please."

"Why?"

"I'm stuck. There's been a war, I can't leave this future. The fabric has changed."

"Then how are you here?"

"This isn't me, or at least not the me you saw yesterday. But this is the reason I will die, or did die, of cancer."

"I don't understand."

A flash of anger in his eyes. "You don't need to understand. Just meet me at the head of the Mill Creek Trail at twelve noon, ten years from today. And bring a good calculator, a good HP scientific."

"If there's a war, how do you know I will be alive to be there?"

"You've already been there. That's why I'm able to be here."

"And if I don't show?"

"Then I die there, and not here." He gestures at the bed, and his body is no longer there. Then he disappears and is replaced with the diseased version of himself. Fading in and out of my vision. "You can't bury me," coughs, "this way, son."

"Fuck. Fine."

The old one goes to the bed and lies down, closes his eyes and stops breathing. The other comes back. "Don't forget."

"Like you didn't forget me?"

I now see pain in his eyes. That cut deep, and I can see him start to retort, catch himself, hold it back. "Ten years. Please."

He goes away again. Too much. My father has left me four times in two days.

Everything around me loses focus, and the tubes and machines seem to become a beast that has come to suck the life-force from my father's silent body. I howl in anguish, and two nurses rush in. One quietly holds my elbow while the other takes the dangling tubes from my hand. I realize I have ripped them from his body.

The tears flow again, far more than any time before.

He was right about the war. Canada and the States take lots of refugees now, but only from Europe. The size of my city has swollen to number in the millions, food is harder to get, almost no one travels by car.

They say it is still a democracy; I think it is a police state. Curfews, elections that don't matter, soldiers on every street corner. But we are still alive.

The appointed day has come. The calculator I bought four years ago, before such luxuries disappeared forever. I also bring a bottle of wine, hoping to perhaps share it with my father. Over the course of these hard years I have forgiven him his sins against me.

I'm early, so I sit on an old bench and wait. The park I am in is still green, after a fashion. The path is paved, but aspen, bushes and weeds choke the sides, and every so often there is a spruce. Different foliage from when I was a child, but they are all that will grow here now.

Some people say the parkland is a luxury, but it is one thing our leaders have not budged on. We were once famous for our green space, and I think the doddering old-timers who now run our lives remember those days with a certain amount of affection.

Two soldiers walk by, eyeing me warily. But their rifles stay down, and they continue their patrol without stopping to question me. I see one whisper something to the other and they both laugh, casting a parting glance my way.

Finally, after perhaps a half hour he steps out of some bushes.

"Father."

He looks startled. "Why are you here?"

I offer him the calculator. "You came to me, said you were stuck here because of the war."

"War?"

I nod. "Nuclear, in the Middle East."

He turns the calculator on, does some quick calculations. "Can I have this?"

I nod. He puts it in his coat pocket.

I offer him the bottle of wine, intending to suggest we share it. He takes it, looks at it, says "Thanks," and disappears.

I stand at the trail head, dismayed. "Father!" I shout, "Don't leave me again!"

But he's gone.

"There was no war."

"What do you mean?" I have introduced this man to the nurse as my nephew. He is fresh-faced at nineteen, still two years away from becoming a father.

"I mean that you remember it because of your connection with me, but it didn't happen."

"How?" The medication adds to my perplexity.

"I changed the equations. Had to."

"Why?"

"I wouldn't be able to travel, otherwise. No one around you remembers it. It faded away for good, and was replaced by other emergencies and tragedies."

"But what about my life? Where did everything go?"

"Still the same. Only, people have begun to find different reasons for the choices that have been made over the years."

This is a sobering thought. Even with the evidence of my father's travels, I had thought certain things were immutable. Was I so drastically wrong?

"What does this do to my work?"

"Nothing. Everything else stays the same. The changes I am able to make are very localized, and take much subjective, objective, and imaginary time to take place. And this is the only one I have ever made that affected more people than myself."

I try to think of more questions, but the meds in my system are making this all very hard to grasp. At least, I think it's the drugs.

He takes the opportunity afforded by the silence to open his shoulder bag and pulls out two crystal glasses and a bottle of wine that looks familiar. He pours the wine, rests the glasses on the bed table. "Here. Let me help you sit up."

Tubes get in the way, but he gets me up. For a moment my bedroom spins around, but it settles down soon enough. When I found I was ill I insisted on home-nursing, rather than an impersonal hospital.

The insurance company had balked, but I have spent my years wisely, cultivating friendships with many who now lead this newly independent northern land. A word from one of them, and my apartment was readied for my dying. It makes it easier to turn away visitors, too, but the young man here today is special.

He puts a straw in my glass, holds it for me to take a sip. "Mmm. Very good. How old is it?"

He thinks for a second. "Can't really say. Somewhere between five years and two hundred, I think."

I remember the wine now. Tears come to my eyes. "I'm glad you came back."

I stretch out my hand and stroke his face. The look of my weathered hand on his skin is jarring, and I remember where I am.

"Join me," he says.

I cough, spitting some of the wine back up. He holds a cloth napkin to my mouth, and it comes away pink, even though the wine is white. The nurse looks in, sternly. "How?" I ask.

"It's easy," he replies. "Just lie down and close your eyes. I'll go get you elsewhen."

The tears rush back. The joy I feel is almost painful. My father wants me with him! After so many years that I thought he wanted to be away from me.

He's crying, too. "I missed you, son. I wasn't a very good dad."

"It's okay. I spent a long time being angry with you, but I think I finally came to my own reconciliation."

"Is all this why you never had a family?"

A good question. I gesture for him to help me lie back down while I think on it. He seems content to let me be quiet as I think, and I hear no sounds of impatience from him. Eventually I say, "Probably. You're very wise for someone who only looks nineteen."

This makes him laugh; a boisterous sound that brings back a flood of visions. Tears well up in my eyes again. At least the lousy disease hasn't dried me out.

"You know I'm not really nineteen."

I nod. I spent much of my life trying to understand the physics involved, even going so far as to go back to university and getting a doctorate. One of few that the government still allows complete studies in.

My work did much for me, and I hope it did much for the world at large. And I became important enough that people began to listen to me, and with my help some libertarians started to find their way into public office again. Perhaps my contributions will eventually make it easier for personal freedoms to become important again.

But I never could figure out how my father avoided the conventional pitfalls of paradox, as well as the unconventional ones that dogged my work for so many years. Maybe now I can find out.

"Where will we go?"

He smiles. "You name it. The universe will be ours."

I smile in return, and hope my toothless grin doesn't scare him away. "It's a deal."

Then I close my eyes and slip away.

I am nineteen, and I have a small backpack packed, but I don't know why. My father comes into the room. "Son, I have someone I'd like you to meet."

Then my father walks into the room, only he's young, younger than I ever knew as a child. He stands beside the father I know, the father who after my mother died always spent so much time away from me, and suddenly I remember!

I remember it all, the meetings, my father's death, the war. Even my own death. A wave of relief washes over me, as I realize that I am being given a new chance at discovering my father and my relationship with him.

"You ready?"

I nod so hard I give myself a headache. "Yes!"

They both hug me, something I'm not used to from my father, then they hug each other.

My older father holds my shoulders for a minute, staring into my eyes. "You be careful son, but enjoy yourself."

All of this affection stuns me. "I wish you could come too."

Both of them laugh. "I already have," he says, "and I already am."

I still don't understand, but perhaps with time, as it were, I will.

"Where are we going?" I ask.

"We'll go say goodbye to yourself first. Then..." He shrugs his shoulders.

I smile and we go. I wonder where else I've already been.

Candas bought what is still probably my best-known (what Peter Watts calls my signature) short story, "The History of Photography,"

but instead you're getting my first published story, "Father Time,"
initially published in Tesseracts 4. Before I was a published author I
was an employee at the late great Greenwoods' Bookshoppe in Ed-
monton, and Candas was a regular customer. We already knew each
other through my involvement with ConText '89, and she knew I want-
ed to write, so one day she stopped at the counter to invite me to take
her university-affiliated spec fic writing course. I did so, and very
much enjoyed it. Shortly after, my first wife and I parted ways, and
Candas knew I was in a bad state of mind, and so when Mike Skeet
and Lorna Toolis decided to buy "Father Time," Candas found out
ahead of time and asked if she could phone and give me the news,
knowing it would cheer me up. I will never forget the gesture.

ROBERT RUNTÉ

SPLIT DECISION

So Mr. Shakey came over the intercom saying it was 2:03 and would all the teachers stop whatever they were doing and please water the plants? As Mrs. Harness went for the door, Bethany-Anne reached over from her desk and peeked out under the shutters.

Mr. Shakey? Oh, sorry. Mr. Sheckley, the principal. But we call him 'Mr. Shakey', because sometimes his judgement is kind of off. Like, that has to be the lamest code phrase ever. I mean, I ask you: if you're in the school intent on a killing rampage and you hear "drop everything and water the plants" over the PA, wouldn't you at least suspect that that means "go to lockdown"? Because you have to know a lockdown is the logical response to your being there, with a rifle; whereas it makes no sense to interrupt class just to water the plants. And Mr. Shakey orders "plant watering" like every other day, because he is totally paranoid.

What? No, no. Nobody had a rifle. I'm just saying it's lame, that's all. So Mr. Sheckley says about watering the plants, and right away Bethany-Anne sneaks the bottom of the shutters up—

What? No, the shutters were down already, before the announce- ment, because Mrs. Harness had us doing this frog on the Smartboard. So, anyway, Bethany-Anne is leaning—

What? Okay, okay. Because our class gets the sun in the afternoon, and you can't see a thing on the Smartboard, even if you're right up front, with the shutters up. We have one of the old-style boards, where the projector hangs down from the top? It's so old, it just totally washes out in direct sunlight. But Mrs. Harness says it will be like another three years before she can even *apply* for them to do an upgrade for our room, but we'll all be graduated by then, so just too bad for us, eh?

So they were down, right, because of the frog? The shutters, I mean. So Bethany-Anne, reaches over—

Frog. The dissection you have to do in Science 7? Gramps says in his day they did real frogs, which is just barbaric. I can't believe that was ever *legal*, let alone something you *had to do* in school. Where was the SPCA? Where was PETA when this was going on? Now you just do it on your slate. But why even *simulate* a dissection? Sure, somebody—some scientist dude—had to do that the first time, once, to find out. But why would you want to keep *re*-doing it? If I want to know what's connected to which, I can just look it up.

But anyway, Mrs. Harness was showing us all on the Smartboard first, before our doing it individual on our slates, and the shutters are down, and Mr. Shakey comes over the PA. Clear?

So when Mrs. Harness goes for the door, Bethany-Anne reaches over and flips the shutters to see if she can see anybody skulking around outside, and right away she spots it.

Sorry? Well, mostly that's true. But the shutter on Bethany-Anne's row is missing the bottom slat, so if you kinda work your hand into the gap, and twist the roller, you can get the bottom four or five slats to all rotate, and you can get a pretty good look outside. Of course, Mrs. Harness goes all freaky if she catches you at it, and you have to listen to her go on and on about how someone could get a shot in, but I mean, how realistic is that? That they would happen to be focused on that particular window the exact moment you happened to flip the slats? And then there is still the whole question of getting the shot through the opening. Because four or five slats is okay to see *out*, but you can't really see *in* from more than—I don't know—a couple of feet away, maybe? It could be done, I guess, with a good scope, but it would have to be someone who knew what they were doing, deliberate, calm, and that's hardly ever what you're up against with your typical lockdown. I think Mrs. Harness is more worried we'll spot a flasher or something. Like we haven't all seen everything there is to see like a million times before on our slates. Last week: Justin forgot to close a window after break, and left it running in the background, and when Mrs. Harness asked him to flip his math to the Smartboard, guess what popped up! I thought Mrs. Harness was going to blow an artery for sure, that time. Though, you know, I was kind of disappointed in Justin. Why do guys always want to watch that kind of stuff? I mean, we get like fifteen minutes for break, and instead of actually *talking* to one of the girls next to him, he spends it watching something like—

Oh, right. Sorry. So anyway, Bethany-Anne makes this kind of a sound that is, you know, not quite a scream, and not a choke exactly, but the kind of sound where you just *know* something is seriously up. So Todd pushes her aside and sticks *his* head to the glass and he's just kind of glued there, even though Mrs. Harness is already half way back from the door and shouting at him to "get down this second". So the rest of us start crowding in, in the hopes of a quick glimpse before Mrs. Harness gets there, and the crowding slows her down quite a bit, so most of us are able to get an okay look at it, sitting right out there in the rink.

Then Mrs. Harness orders everyone to the far wall, and she starts tipping tables over and telling everyone to get into crash position behind their desks; only that is so obviously lame! It just makes no sense to me. It's like, well, if it's going to blow, what exactly do you expect a set of shutters and a couple of tipped over student desks to do about it? We looked pathetic. I didn't want people seeing me like that. Because by now half the kids have their cells out and are phoning EMS, or their folks; and the other half are uploading video of the first half, who are cowering there like morons.

And we were already way beyond 'locked door' as the appropriate response here. Because if they've got interstellar travel down, a locked door is probably not going to deter them. So either we should all be moving out the opposite exit as fast as our feet could carry us, or we should just relax and go greet our new masters from Megnar 7, or wherever.

So I go over to the fire exit and start leaning on the crashbar. Casual, you know? Not making a production of it. Like I was just thinking maybe of leaning out for a quick look. But I had already figured it as pretty safe.

Well, no, I didn't mean 'safe' exactly. Obviously, this was not a normal situation. I understand your point there. I'm just saying that if something were going to explode, it probably would have done that already, when it came down. But none us had even heard a thing. And I know for sure I had my earbuds out when it must have come down. Because it certainly hadn't been there at break, and I hadn't exactly been in a hurry to tune into Mrs. Harness putting that poor frog down—simulated or not—so my ears were still naked right up to Mr. Sheckley's announcement. I definitely would have heard *something* if that had been a crash out there. So if it wasn't a crash, then no 'kaboom', right?

Oh. I didn't know that. Well, I'm just telling you what I was thinking at the time. Just let me finish here, or I'll get all jumbled up. So I'm saying, I didn't think we were in any danger from the *ship* aspect of it. I mean, it pretty much looked like it had landed there in one piece as intended.

But on the other hand, if I were flying around the galaxy, and I wanted to put down on Earth, the hockey rink of Allan Wilson Middle School would not necessarily be my first choice, you know? So either it was some kind of mistake or accident, or emergency landing kind of deal; or, this was part of like a much larger fleet, and they were landing everywhere with so many ships that there was even one to spare for Prairie Creek. And if that were the case—well, like I said, time to meet our new masters, and here's hoping they aren't into eating our brains.

But I figured, you have interstellar flight, you probably have to be like some kind of way advanced civilization, and that probably implies a certain level of vegetarianism when it comes to intelligent species. Assuming that we qualify.

So, I figured, probably they were having some kind of problem, and the polite thing—the civilized thing to do—would be for someone to go and ask, you know, if they needed anything.

So I am starting to lean on the crashbar a little harder, when I hear this clop clop clop coming up fast behind me, which I know to be Sarah's clogs without having to turn around, so I wait a second for her to get there, and she whispers, "What are you doing?"; only, you know, her tone is more like, "What, *are you crazy*?!" And so I say, "I figure they're probably not here to eat our brains" and she says, "Well, duh. But what about radiation?"

So I ease up on the crashbar again, because this thought has given me pause. This is precisely why Sarah is my best friend. Because more than once she has thought of something that I have maybe missed. "An advanced civilization," I said, working it through with her, but still whispering so as not to attract Mrs. Harness's attention, "would probably include safety regulations. With regard to acceptable levels of radiation."

"Well, yeah" Sara whispers back, "But the number one safety rule would be, 'no landing on Earth' and the second rule would be, 'no landing in school hockey rinks'. So probably something went wrong already."

I see her point. So I ask, "Okay, maybe radiation. What then?"

And she says, "Shielding or distance. Assuming always we haven't already taken a fatal dose."

I look over at everybody still huddled behind their desks and kind of nod in that direction, and ask, "Any good?"

"Maybe if we covered the desks in layers of aluminum foil from the cafeteria," Sarah tells me, "but wood is useless."

"Distance?" I ask her.

"Levels decrease with the square of the distance."

"My basement?"

She nodded. "We could still see okay from there, but would be nearly three times further away. Radiation would be only a tenth whatever it is here. And cement is good. "

Well, I don't know; they never said. I'm just telling you what Sarah told me.

So then I looked over to where Mrs. Harness was still under her desk, and there was no way she was going to unlock the door to the hallway. Mrs. Harness is not a half-bad teacher, but she is not one for taking initiative. She sticks pretty much to the curriculum, whether simulated dissections make sense or not. So if Mr. Sheckley had called for a lockdown, we were going to stay locked in until the 'all-clear'.

"Okay," I said, "we make a run for my house," and slammed my elbow into the crashbar. I saw Mrs. Harness bang her head when the exit alarm went off, but we were out and pelting along the side of the school before she could even crawl out from under her desk. I was pretty much just focused on making it around the corner of the school, and could hear the clacking of Sarah's clogs keeping up with me, so I didn't look back at all, and I didn't immediately recognize that the grinding sound was the saucer splitting opening, and so neither of us saw the ramp coming out of it until it was nearly on top of us.

So I hit the brakes and pull back, but Sarah plows into me and kind of knocks me, and I'm on the ramp, teetering, and Sarah's all, "What are you *doing*?!" and I'm looking back at her in disbelief because it's not *my* fault I'm on the ramp, *she's* the one who knocked me, but then it penetrates that they've opened up and I'm thinking, "wait" and I point at the ramp and say, "No radiation!" and Sarah's looking at me, and I explain that they wouldn't open up if there was a radiation leak or whatever, and Sarah's all, "You don't know that! Maybe they're just not affected by it!" But I figure, they're kind of inviting us in, and that wouldn't make sense if the radiation was going to kill us, so it's gotta be okay.

I look back at the school and I notice the shutters are like a quarter of the way up in Ms. Rossiter's class, and there are like forty arms sticking cells out the bottom, filming me and Sarah, waiting to see what we do. Or whether something comes out with a deathray or whatever. So I take like maybe half a step up the ramp, when Sarah shouts, "Viruses!" and I pause again, but just for a second this time, because I remember Mrs. Harness telling us how our dogs don't catch our colds and vice versa, and dogs are practically family compared to whatever is in *there*, so I just shake my head, and say "I doubt we're that compatible" and keep going. And Sarah does this exasperated little stomp with her clogs, and says, "You don't know that!" So I stop, because she's not wrong. But I tell her, "They've got the ship, so I'm guessing they're brainy enough to have thought it all through." Only she says, "You can't know that!" again. And she's right of course, but I just kind of shrug, because, hey, you can never *know*. Not completely, right?

So we're standing, looking at each other, and Sarah says, kind of quiet, "You can't go in there. It would be crazy." Then I just say, "I have a plan", and start going up the ramp again. So Sarah runs after me with her clogs clanging on the ramp, and catches up and asks, "What's the plan?" And I explain, "I'm not going in. I'm stopping half-way up. That way, they'll have to come out and we'll meet half-way." And Sarah says, "That's your plan?" and I say, "Yes," and she says, "That's it? That's not a plan!" And I say, "No, this will work. Because it shows willing, and because, you know, meeting half way is what you do!" And Sarah shouts, "What do you mean, 'That's what you do?' What you *do* is call out the army and the air force!" And I have to stop and give Sarah 'The Look', because, come on! She's been here for like her whole life, almost. "Sarah! That's maybe how

Americans would do it, or maybe your Dad when he was an Airforce Captain back in the Bangladesh, but for crying out loud, you're as Canadian as me. Meeting 'half way' is how Canadians do it!" And then Sarah gives *me* 'The Look' back and says, "You're the one who told me Canadians don't change the lightbulb, they wait for the government to do it." And I wave my arm at the school where all the teachers are hunkered down and say, "Do you see the government anywhere? Look, if they" —I'm pointing up the ramp here —"If they wanted the Army and Air Force and diplomats and world leaders, they would have landed in front of the White House; if they land in back of Allan Wilson Middle School, it's because they just want to do some repairs, maybe, or get directions, or whatever, but the appropriate response is to be neighbourly and offer to help them out, without making a huge deal out of it!"

So then I noticed Sarah isn't saying anything and is looking kind of stressed, so I say, "Sarah?" Because now I'm thinking I was maybe out of line implying she wasn't being Canadian enough. Because she can be sensitive about that: like the time Drew said he thought she looked like 'a foreign princess' in her blue sari with the diamonds. He just meant she looked exotic, but things never come out quite right when Drew says them, and Sara had been totally slammed he'd said 'foreign'. But it wasn't about that this time. She looks at me and says, "So the plan is we only go half way up, right?" And I say, "That's the plan," and Sarah says, "and we stopped about a third of the way up to have this little chat, right?" And right away I get it, because we're already way past the half-way mark, and getting closer to the top every second, even though we've stopped walking, so I just grab her arm and yell, "Run" and we take off for the bottom of the ramp.

The one thing Sarah and I hate most about school is the Ding Test. You know the one? Where this bell goes 'Ding' and you have to keep running as many laps as you can before the next 'Ding'. It's so stupid and demeaning. With Sarah's lungs and my ankles, it's just torture.

And what's it for, exactly? When do you ever need to run like that and keep running until you actually fall down from exhaustion?

That's what I was thinking as we ran for it and kept running and running, as hard as we could, but didn't seem to be making any progress towards the bottom. But instead of a 'ding', there was this sort of collective groan from the school windows as Sarah started to flag.

Then the fire exit to Mrs. Harness' room crashes open, and Justin and Drew came pounding out. Todd came out too, but just far enough to grab the door and drag it closed again. I didn't know what they were doing at first, and wanted to warn them away, but I didn't have the breath or the nerve to stop running; and frankly, if they were stupid enough to come *out* when they saw us coming *back,* that was their own look out.

But after a second, I realized they were headed for the ramp and for us.

Say what you want, but those guys can *run.* They hit the ramp in a blur, and were racing up to meet us fast, faster than any relay race I've ever seen them do, and I was worried for a second that they were going to crash right into us as we were trying to get away—only that never happened. Sarah and I kept running down at best speed, and they were racing up—I mean, really sprinting it!—but somehow the distance between us didn't shrink at all. On the contrary, space started to slowly expand, stretching out between us, until it became obvious that we were never going to reach each other.

Justin must have seen it too, because he started undoing his belt; he almost stumbled yanking it out while still running, head down and coming on like a fullback, and then flung it at me. I kinda ducked at first, but on his second throw I got what he was doing and I grabbed for it. I caught it on the third throw, by sort of lunging at it like in volleyball, and then I was tumbling past Justin, and Justin was shooting past me up the ramp.

I was still holding the belt with Justin on the other end, so kind of pivoted to get myself up and standing again, dug in my heels, and yanked him back towards me, now that I was closer to the bottom of the ramp than he was; he spun around and crashed into Sarah and Drew, who were both behind me, which left me disoriented because Sarah had been higher up the ramp and Drew lower, so I couldn't figure out how any of that was happening. Then I saw that we were all of us very nearly at the top, and moving inside, but before I could shout a warning, Justin was pulling me with the belt towards the edge, and shouted "Jump!"

But it's way too late, and next thing we know, we're all inside.

Justin and I jumping? Yeah, we saw that too. Which was pretty weird for us, but we were already inside by then, so we were kind of preoccupied with that. It was only later that they explained it was just the 4% of us that reacted fast enough that had jumped. But I remember thinking at the time, man, that must have *hurt!* Because we were pretty high up by then, I'm telling you!

So anyway, we're inside and right away it's just like that movie— the original, I mean, not the remake—because everything is this kind of gloomy black and white, and it's kind of hard to make anything out, and I'm like half expecting Gort to step out of the shadows; but of course it wasn't like that at all, once we got the goggles.

Sure they gave us goggles. Why wouldn't they? Because, as I'm trying to explain, everything is virtual with them, so without the colors, it's just blank walls. Nothing to see at all. Like trying to watch TV with the picture off. You've got to have the goggles.

To see the colors. Because our eyes don't see in the same range, and the goggles adjust for that.

I'm not sure exactly. Early that first day, sometime. Within a couple of hours, I guess. Because things only started to make sense once we got the goggles and could see what's going on.

Well, that's a lot harder to judge. I mean, it's not like they had a big clock up anywhere. Oh, and our watches didn't work. Sarah and Drew both had watches on, but they were both frozen at 2:19. The watches, I mean, not Sarah and Drew. Same with Justin and my cells.

And you can't phone out, though I guess that's obvious. So, I'd have to guess a couple of days. Four maybe. Though now you come to say it, it's funny, because we never got hungry or had to sleep or anything.

Yeah, yeah! That's it! That's exactly what *they* said: "subjectivity of time". Something about how you "can't master faster than light travel without first mastering the subjectivity of time". I don't pretend to get all that; Sarah's the science geek.

Well, no, not 'said'. I know I said 'said', but mostly it was writing. On the walls. Texting, you know? Sarah says she thinks they're deaf because they never tried talking to us, so maybe they don't use sound that way? But then *I* said they must be blind too, because they never used pictures either, but Drew said that was really stupid. Anyway, it became obvious pretty early on that they were asking if we wanted to go with them. Like be exchange students. And from the second they said it, I was beside myself with indecision. Because part of me really *really* wanted to. I mean, you know, the whole "boldly go where none have gone before" thing, right? That's pretty wild! But of course, another part of me wanted to stay right here. Keep my regular life. Go for the theater, instead. Because Mr. Bartain says I have a real shot. A *real* shot. And I've worked hard for that. And I'd miss Kasia, my little sister. And my folks.

But then I'd think, I would not miss Allan Wilson Middle School. Okay, Mr. Bartain, maybe. But seriously, I've got what, another year of middle school and another *three* of high school and then who knows how many of university? I think my Dad lived his whole life practically before he finally graduated. I wouldn't have to do any of that. I could start my life *now*; I could leave with them *now,* and have the adventure of a lifetime; of a hundred lifetimes!

But then I'd realize I didn't have Bear-Bear and Socks with me, and how could I stand to leave them behind? And it would like, *kill* mom. Dad would get it, sort of: me leaving in a saucer would be cool for him. But he'd probably say that out loud, and then mom would kill *him!*

I wasn't even clear if we got to say 'goodbye' or anything, because when they tried to explain that bit, it wasn't very clear at first. I couldn't imagine what my folks would think, what my little sister would think, if they saw me get in the saucer, and the saucer took off, and then not knowing if I was okay. I couldn't do that to them. But then, they said that wouldn't be an issue, and I shouldn't worry about that when I made my final decision, so then I'd flip again.

I kept going back and forth, and every time I did, I'd end up arguing with myself again. That part was definitely weird. Though also strangely reassuring. You really get to know yourself, to understand what it is you *really* want when you have to work through a decision like that. A life-changing decision.

I think Sarah got it faster than the rest of us. What it would really mean. Because her folks had to make that decision coming to Canada.

And then there was the whole Justin thing. A lot of Justin really wanted to go, but only if I would go with him. That really kind of freaked me. Because, I had just never thought of Justin that way before. So at some point we noticed we were talking about Justin almost as much as about the decision, and I said, "Look, Justin is not the question. Justin stays or goes, but either way, he's going to *be there* so we can worry about that another time; there will be lots of opportunities to sort out how I feel about Justin later. The only question is: what do *I* want to do." I have to say, I was a little proud of myself for saying that, because I could hear my mom always telling me, you should never make a decision based just on what some boy wants. And this was a perfect example of that. So I dug around and found some receipts in my jacket pocket, and a pen, and used the scraps to write down my decision, and I told Justin to write down his, and the others, so that we all made our own decision without worrying about what the others were planning. And that made it a bit scarier, not knowing if anyone was coming with you, or if you stayed behind, whether they would all go off on an adventure without you. But that was the only way to be sure it was our own, independent choice.

Of course, as I sat down to write my answer, I probably flipped flopped a thousand times again. But in the end, I had something written on the paper, and I put it down on the floor in front of me, and the others had too. And then we all sat there for a minute, all of us, thinking about what we had done. And then they said it was time to go, so we all went our separate ways.

And here I am.

I got the impression they were really pleased with the way things turned out, too. That we had all made such thoughtful, deliberate decisions. And of course, because all four of us were so ambivalent about it all, it ties up all the loose ends for them pretty neatly too!

Sorry? What? Oh, I just meant, that it doesn't look like 'Alien Abduction' if the people who go in come out again. Because if we had all chosen to go, like unanimous, then I guess they'd have some explaining to do! Though I gather, that doesn't come up very often.

Sorry? What don't you...? Because a lot of me wanted to go, of course. I was pretty evenly divided on this one. Almost completely down the middle. They told me in the end about 49% went, and 51% stayed. With Justin, it was closer to 90/10. I mean, 90% wanting to go. What do you suppose that says about Justin? Do you think that means he's terribly unhappy with his life here? Because that could be a problem if...you know, something were to happen with Justin and me. Or does it just mean he's into adventure? That could be okay.

Sarah came out about 40% going and 60% staying. She told me that after all her parents went through to get her here, she would have felt bad choosing somewhere else; though of course the ones that went felt differently. I shouldn't say this, but I think some of them chose to go because I did. Sarah and me make a pretty good team. I can't even guess where Drew comes into it with Sarah, though. For or against, I couldn't begin to tell you.

What are you talking about? No, that's not it at all. Look, you're completely missing it. Let me start again. Every time you make a decision, every time you choose to open the door or not to, the universe splits: in one continuum you opened the door, in the other you didn't. They explained it to us just like that. So, normally, you're just you and you opened the door and go through; or you're the you that didn't, but you still just go on with your life from that point, maybe wondering, maybe not, what your life would have been had you made the other choice. Right? Every decision is like that. Every one.

But what if you were in a place where you could see the split coming? What if every time you had a choice, you had the chance to see both continuums stretching out in front of you, the door open and the door closed, and both of you poised to make the choice? And you could talk to the other you, and debate which was the right choice, discuss the pros and cons? Maybe, switch sides. Choose the other option instead this time.

But then, as the other you makes a point, part of you decides to go with that option, and part of you sticks with your original choice—so you split again, between the you that was convinced to change, and the one that wasn't. And then there's a friend with you, who offers to go with you if you choose the first option; and you're torn, so suddenly there's two more of you. Except by now your friend is having second thoughts, so there are two of him, and so part of you wonders if your friend will see it through, so you split again. And, well, you see how it works. Pretty soon, there are an awful lot of you sitting around debating, and some of you wander off topic and start talking about Justin. But in the end, you have to make your decision. And some of you go through the door, and some of you don't.

Some of us—some of me—went with the saucer, and some of us didn't. So they get the exchange students they wanted; and Mom and Dad and Kasia get me back safe and sound. Everybody wins.

Nope. No regrets. None at all. What's to regret? That's the real beauty of it all: because, of course, that part of me that would have regretted not going, went.

The story, Split Decision, came to me listening to Tigana, my then 13-year-old daughter, breathlessly trying to explain something that had happened at school that day. I kept having to interrupt to untangle what she was saying, because she assumed her audience familiar with the background context, which we weren't. And I thought, what if there had been a real emergency, and she had to explain what happened to someone in authority?

Tigana may have been my inspiration for "Split Decision", but it was Candas Jane Dorsey who taught me to listen to those around me, not just for story ideas, but more importantly, to hear the nuances of speech and tone and rhythm and relationship. I don't think I would have 'heard' that story without Candas' mentorship; I certainly wouldn't be an author or editor today had I not had Candas as a role model.

To take just one example, by allowing me to shadow her for a day to see how real writers lived and worked, Candas taught me the importance of pacing oneself, of work/life balance, and of "stopping on the clock, not on a block" (as I later explained the principle to my students). When my writing still stalled, she made a housecall to diagnose the problem at my keyboard. Seeing me obsessively revising every line as I wrote it, she reached over and turned off the monitor. "Now write," she said. I almost had a breakdown on the spot—how could I know what to write next, if I couldn't see and revise what I had just written? But Candas was standing right there, so I had to suck it up and keep writing. By forcing me to write stream of consciousness, Candas' exercise prevented me from both overthinking or overworking my first draft. As I now teach my students, it is a mistake to try to hold your first draft to final-draft standards.

And then there was Candas' workshop on overcoming writer's block. After taking it twice myself, I hosted Candas' workshop for my colleagues and graduate students; and then stole that workshop outright as part of my own repertoire as a thesis supervisor. I'm still handing out Candas' advice (http://www.essentialedits.ca/EEthesis.htm) twenty years on.

But most of all, I admired Candas' courage in following her passion for writing, even at the cost of not always knowing where her next paycheck was coming from, or having to drive a Volvo so decrepit it seemed part of the zombie apocalypse. She taught me—and a hundred other Albertans—that instead of running off to greener pastures in some distant metropolis, you stayed where you were and fought to create the community you wanted to be part of. She demonstrated how to have the daring to be the writer, the editor, the teacher—the publisher even—that one's community needs to give it voice. She dared to pull herself up by her own bootstraps . . . and brought the rest of us with her.

CANDAS JANE DORSEY: A FRIENDSHIP SPANNING 40+ YEARS

In 1975, I was a university student living in Edmonton, and attending the U. of Alberta to complete my Diploma in Education. I had recently discovered the feminist movement, and was eager to learn more. One day I picked up the November-December 1974 issue of a locally-produced magazine devoted to feminism and its emerging relationship to the arts, culture, and to the political landscape in Canada. The smiling and confident faces of the women on the cover got my attention, and I had to get to know them.
http://awmp.athabascau.ca/documents/November-December%201974.pdf

So I contacted them, and to my delight, was told by their editor, Susan McMaster, that I'd be welcome to attend one of their meetings and perhaps even get involved with the production of issues of *Branching Out*.

I began attending their regular planning sessions and business meetings, gladly taking on the role of Secretary and recorder. I did a bit of fiction editing as well. When each issue was in production, I learned the ins and outs of layout, in a pre-desktop publishing era. Carefully (using a very sharp blade) slicing up strips of copy received

from the type-setter, and gluing them to a large template with extremely smelly, and probably toxic rubber cement. Those were the
days.

You can see Candas' first appearance in *Branching Out* as an author in this link.
http://awmp.athabascau.ca/documents/January-
February%201975.pdf where her story, "Sally Go 'Round the
Roses" appears.

Some issues after that, Candas joined the Collective briefly as a
Fiction editor. So I guess I have officially known her since late in
1975. From 1976 to 1977 I took a break when I secured a teaching job
in Stettler, a town in central Alberta. I re-joined *Branching Out* upon
my return to Edmonton, although Candas had moved on to other pursuits by then.

Then I got involved in the local Science Fiction and Fantasy fan
community. One of our more ambitious projects was the formation of
a new SF convention called NonCon, which had its inaugural run in
the fall of 1978. We modelled the programming after V-Con, a convention in Vancouver that many of us had attended, and were happy to
copy. And one of the things we had was a fiction contest.

As the only "English teacher" in the crowd, I was put in charge of
the contest (we had a team of judges already selected). One short story
manuscript had an author name familiar to me, and I was pleased to
see Candas' name after a long absence. To make a long story shorter,
her story was ultimately selected as the winning entry, and for all I
know, this may have been her first foray at writing SF&F.

Our reunion was brief that weekend, and our paths did not cross
again until a couple of years later when I joined the Writers Guild of
Alberta. I started volunteering for more and more Guild activities, and
served on the Board of the WGA during Candas' Presidency. Her
stature in the Alberta writing community and her power as a most articulate spokesperson for the arts in Alberta continued to grow.

She also grew and appeared to make her home as a writer of SF, and we'd meet at SF conventions every year. In 1989, two significant things happened. The national organization of writers and editors of Canadian SF, known as SF Canada, had its inaugural meeting at a convention in Edmonton. And some of my fellow writers and I decided to start publishing *On Spec*, because Canadian SF writers needed a market that "got" them.

We all agreed that Candas Jane Dorsey was an ideal person to have as part of our first Editorial Advisory Board. She'd read and comment on stories that we selected from the slushpile, and contributed to the high quality of fiction we were publishing.

Since that time, Candas has been a strong advocate of Canadian SF writing and of women's writing and creativity. She fights for respect and recognition of marginalized people and communities, and is fiercely loyal to her friends. I'm proud to be one of them.

FAVOURITE RECENT CANDAS MEMORY? Probably the chilly fall afternoon a few years ago, when my daughter, Danica and I spent several hours in the back yard of a rental property owned by Candas and Timothy, making numerous attempts to net a dozen or more very reluctant goldfish from an extremely muddy backyard pond. Hilarity ensued.

BEST THING ABOUT CANDAS? Her aforementioned loyalty and friendship, and the fact that pretty much everything she says is well-thought out and totally intelligent, articulate and memorable.

SISTER MARGARET

"Charmaine?" My voice echoed around the chamber, adding to the prickling feeling of unease that had settled around my shoulders like a scarf the instant I walked into the temple.

She turned slowly, sinuously. Dark purple robes fluttered around her, gradually drifting back to her sides like leaves caught in a sudden updraft and then forsaken. Her unfathomable blue eyes drilled into me. If I live a hundred years, I'll never see another pair of eyes like hers. They were the bright blue of a hot flame, and they seared me to my soul.

"It's Margaret now." I noticed her voice didn't reverberate through the chilly air like mine, but then her eyes drew my attention, and nothing else mattered. "Sister Margaret."

That's right; she was Sister Margaret now, a priestess in the order of Rakkir. Of course, it didn't matter what she called herself. Margaret, Leif, or Fairy-Dumpling, she'd always be Charmaine to me.

We'd had less than ideal childhoods. We'd confided in each other and shared our pain. Then, when she turned thirteen, Charmaine ran away from home and became a whore. When I asked her about it, she said she might as well get paid for it because someone or another had been taking it for free for years. Poor Charmaine, I couldn't even imagine dealing with that. We lost contact soon after that because my father took to beating me extra hard if he heard I'd been seen with her.

After several beatings, I stayed away. Even though I'd done it against my will, I continued to torment myself for deserting her.

Hell of a way to treat a friend.

I guess it must have been five years later that she found religion and abandoned her name to become Margaret. Sister Margaret became an institution in Haven: a priestess of the God of Deception. She made it her mission to aid other street children and bring them in out of the cold, as it were. Cynics said she merely wanted to boost the number of Rakkir's followers. I think part of her motivation was to help those who were as lost as she had been.

"...didn't hear a word I said, did you, Michael?"

Her sharp words and the sound of my name brought me out of my reverie. Tearing my gaze from her eyes, I studied a statue over her left shoulder.

"Of course I was listening. You need me to take care of a pimp who is harassing one of your girls." I'd taken a guess, a wild shot in the dark, but some God was looking out for me because my aim proved true—this time.

"Yes. Xaphan has been terrorizing all the girls who work in the Dregs, threatening them with unspeakable consequences if they don't work for him and hand over most of what they make each night."

She paused, looking at me to make sure my mortification matched hers, so I sculpted my face into a mask of outrage and held her gaze while spitting, "That bastard."

Of course, I did think him a bastard for using the whores that way, but I didn't see why Charmaine involved herself. Surely there had been a lot of pimps who'd come and gone over the years, but she'd never called on me before, never requested my services.

"What's so special about this one, Char...Margaret?" I wanted to hear her say it, though I already suspected the answer. Xaphan had made quite a name for himself. I knew what he was, and Charmaine must as well. After twenty years, you don't ask the childhood friend who turned his back on you to deal with a pimp. The question remained: would she tell me about it? Forewarned is forearmed, so they say. Would she arm me or send me out after this creature, assuming him to be merely another man?

"He's brutal. He's murdered at least two girls because they refused to pay him for protection, and he's kidnapped one of my girls who left the streets to join the Order."

Ah, true to her God and his teachings, Charmaine wasn't going to tell me all she knew; she would let me find out for myself. I wondered then if she realized the sort of danger she was sending me into on her behalf. After one look at her steely blue eyes, I knew that she did. She knew, and a part of her probably wanted me to perish at this creature's hands—the part that was still furious at me for abandoning her so many years ago.

I understood; a part of me remained rather pissed about it too. If only I'd stood up to my father a few years sooner, maybe then I could have talked her off the streets. Who knows how many beatings I'd have saved her, how many men she could have avoided sleeping with. Who knows what would have happened if I'd had the guts to tell the old man no and mean it. So no, I didn't blame her, but that wasn't going to make the job any easier.

"Okay, Margaret. I'll do it."

I thought I saw a flicker in her eyes—fear, perhaps, or relief. Whatever it was, she quickly masked it once more. You don't serve the God of Lies without learning a thing or two about keeping secrets.

She nodded, pulled her robes tighter against herself and knelt at the altar to complete her prayers. As I moved to go, I noticed how the candles around her made my shadow flicker and morph as it crossed the floor. It shifted with each step, at one moment looking positively demonic, at another quite mundane. Strangely enough, when I glanced back over my shoulder at Charmaine, bathed in light from the flickering flames and lost in her prayers, she was wholly bereft of a shadow of her own.

I didn't need to go looking to find Xaphan; I knew exactly where he was. Two decades of hunting creatures like him had given me knowledge no mortal should have nor want. I knew where to find him and how to kill him, but that was the easy part. Catching him at a vulnerable time and getting through his security would be the challenge.

Xaphan was a vampire, a leech. He thrived on misery, survived on blood, and lived for far longer than any human could. He hadn't lived this long through luck, but through skill and attention to detail. Not only would I have to find my way to his resting place, I would have to go through the veritable army of followers he'd set in place to guard him while he slept the daylight hours away.

I'd ended the lives of innumerable men and creatures; if the Gods permitted, I wanted to continue doing so for decades to come. Normally, I'd make a trip to one of my favorite mages, load up on spells and then storm the vampire's residence. A fireball or two would take out all his followers, and you'd be surprised how fast an item enchanted to cast "sunlight" at a word will turn a voracious vampire into a pile of stinking dust. But this time I felt as though I might need more. Something about this Xaphan, and the job in particular, tickled my mind. I wanted to do it right, to make things up to Charmaine. I wanted to help her now, even though I'd been unable to do so then. I think that caused part of my hesitation to do it the usual way—part, but not all.

Rumor on the street was, in addition to surrounding his coffin with followers made loyal to him with promises of immortality, Xaphan used innocent hostages. Charmaine's story about one of her girls gave credence to this tale, and so I hesitated to go in with fireballs blazing. No, this would take more stealth and more weaponry than I alone could provide.

Bayne could be a bit of a barbarian at times; however, he owned the most unbelievable sword you ever saw and wielded it with an unparalleled skill. I knew where to find him; he was as constant as the sun, that one.

I opened the door to Llewellyn's whorehouse and took a quick look around the tap room. Haven was, perhaps, the only city in existence where most anyone could be welcome. Only here could you see elves drinking with dwarves, or reptars drinking with humans. Even so, Bayne was never difficult to spot; even here, he stood out.

He had white hair—not blond like what you might see on a pure human, but as white as bone—and his eyes were an icy blue that made women go weak in the knees. Though he wasn't beefy, I'd seen him heft full-grown men over his head and through windows without breaking a sweat. Rumor said his father was an incubus; if true, that would account for his incredible strength. Then again, how do you ask a man if he's half-demon? Walk up and say, "Hey buddy, you got horns under that creepy colored hair?" Not a good idea, unless you worship the Goddess of Pain. I never did find out how true the rumors were, but it didn't matter: he could swing a sword like no one you'd ever seen, and he worked for cheap if you told him it was for a good cause. Yes, Bayne was the man I needed at my side for this job.

He was currently sitting up on a mound of pillows with a tankard in his hand and a gaggle of giggling whores spread out around his feet like a harem. I didn't have time to admire the view; it was almost midnight, and I intended to strike at dawn.

"Bayne, you up for a job?" My voice cut through the inane chatter of the girls at his feet like a lightning bolt through a tree. He caught my eye and nodded, and I took a seat at the bar and waited for him to disentangle himself from his fan club. After stepping over the girls scattered around him, he swaggered over to me and plopped himself down on the stool at my side.

"What kind of job, Michael?"

Straight to the point; no messing around or lame attempts at chit-chat. Yet another reason why I liked the guy.

"It's a leech."

Bayne's eyebrows shot up and he began to stand. I interrupted his movement by continuing quickly. "You don't have to go near the vampire—that's my part of the job. I need you to take out his minions. I can't use my usual methods because they kill indiscriminately, and there is a good chance he has innocent hostages."

He sat back down, looking at me intently with those ghostly blue eyes of his. Then he nodded.

"You know I won't deal with vampires. The only reason I'm even considering accepting this job is because it's you offering it." He snatched up a toothpick from the bar and started twirling it between his lips. "What's it pay?"

Ah, what's it pay. The question I'd been dreading above all others. Truth be told, Margaret couldn't pay me. Followers of all the main religious orders swear an oath of poverty. Rakkir was no different. Hell, I couldn't have asked her to pay me anyway, even if she could afford it, not after I'd abandoned her when we were kids. I owed her this job.

What's it pay? I'd have offered him cash out of my own pocket if I could, but though I didn't follow any of the Gods, I lived as if I did. Bounty hunting and vampire slaying don't pay nearly as well as you might think.

"What's it pay?" I sighed, and then turned to give Bayne my best look of sincerity. "I'm afraid it pays only whatever you can take off the corpses."

He spat the toothpick out and took a long swig from the tankard in his hand. "Vampire minions? Hell, I could make more robbing a stranger on the street!"

"True, but it's for a good cause."

"What cause? Lining your wallet?"

"No, it's for Sister Margaret." He had a soft spot for whores, and Charmaine was practically their patron saint. I hated manipulating him this way, but I really needed him with me on this job.

"For Sister Margaret, eh? How's she figure into this?"

"The leech, Xaphan, has been charging all her girls for protection. From himself, of course."

Bayne nodded, rolling his eyes. "Of course."

"Well, the girls who can't pay get hurt, or worse, and at least one of them has been abducted."

"I suppose I can take the job, seeing as how it's for a good cause and all. But there is one condition."

I knew what he was going to say—the standard condition everyone placed on a job involving a vampire. All the same, I nodded and lifted a brow to make like I couldn't wait to hear it.

"If I get turned, you need to kill me."

His eyes held my own, their creepy color searing me the way Charmaine's had earlier. His intensity impressed me. No one wants to become a vampire, excepting only their deluded minions.

Bayne stared at me with a forcefulness I'd never seen before. He didn't ask me to kill him if he were turned—he demanded it. I wondered, yet again, what it was with him and vampires; but really, it didn't matter to me. So I nodded and, with as much conviction as I could force into my voice, said, "If you get turned, I'll kill you. I swear."

Several hours later, we stood shivering outside a ramshackle factory while the last seconds of night ticked away. I double-checked my equipment. Because Bayne would be dealing with any mortals on this night, I wasn't carrying much. A collection of sharpened wooden stakes filled the converted quiver on my back, and a big mallet fit snugly into a loop on my belt. I had a pure silver dagger inside another loop, in case monsters other than Xaphan lingered inside, and, of course, my mirror. The mirror was a woman's compact I had paid a mage to enchant. Upon opening, it would cast the spell "sunlight"— light would burst forth from it, harmless to humans but powerful enough to turn even the oldest vampire into a pile of ash in mere seconds. I'd requested the mage put two charges on it, costing me all my money. I figured it would be worth it if something went wrong.

The horizon was tinged with pink when Bayne drew his sword and nodded tersely at me. "You ready?"

I nodded in return and slid my mirror out of my pocket.

"I'll go in first and take care of the people; you stay behind me until we're clear. Once my job is done, I'm out of there. If you really want to find the stinking leech, you're on your own. I'll make sure there are no people to help him out, but there ain't no way in The Abyss I'm going anywhere near him."

"I understand, Bayne." I looked up at the sky and nodded. "Alright, let's go."

Not one to waste time with niceties, Bayne kicked down the door and went to work.

I'd seen him at work with his sword before, plenty of times, each one better than the last, but nothing had prepared me for this.

Xaphan had a lot of minions—a lot. They swarmed on Bayne like flies on shit, a living wave of fists and feet, all determined to bring him down. None of them reached him. His face, contorted by battle fury, looked every bit like a demon, all trace of humanity erased. He moved the sword as though it were an extension of himself, each movement calculated to destroy as many of his foes as possible. Within minutes, the roar of battle subsided to the whimpering of wounded, and Bayne's once white hair was stained pink with blood and gore. An occasional cut ripped through his shirt; one or two even managed to draw blood. But in less than ten minutes, he'd reduced the vampire's army to a pile of mangled corpses and unidentified gore.

I entered as he replaced his sword in the scabbard strapped across his back, careful to watch my step lest I slip on the blood and goo and find myself covered in things I'd rather not contemplate. From a far corner, buried in shadows mortal eyes couldn't hope to penetrate, the distinct sound of feminine sobs could be heard. The leech had hostages after all. Good thing I'd decided against the fireball.

"You get the girls," I said. "I'll take care of the vampire and meet you back outside."

Bayne nodded and delivered a sharp kick to the nose of one of his opponents who lay moaning in the sea of gore. The man's face imploded, shattering beneath the force of Bayne's boot, and then Bayne headed wordlessly toward the sound of the hostages.

I winced inwardly at the brutality of his action, then shrugged it off. In war, shit happens; he couldn't be the best sword for hire in the land if he were squeamish about killing. Nor could he afford to turn his back on an enemy who still drew breath, injured or not.

I watched his back disappear into the darkness and thought about calling out to warn him to watch for traps, but then I thought better of it. Bayne was no fool; he knew what he was doing. I could trust him to get the girls out of the house safely. Now it was up to me to find the vampire and kill him.

Vampires, like most animals, are pretty predictable. And they're paranoid. They like to put their coffins at the lowest, darkest point of the building they are sleeping in, and though they often ward the room with spells, they never let anyone else in it—not even to guard them while they sleep.

I found the stairs with no difficulty; factories, too, are notoriously predictable. Following them down into the dank belly of the building, I kept an eye out for traps. I found two wards outside one door, but they were simple enough to disarm. That's the thing about magic: it's difficult to create, but not tough to sabotage.

I was surprised to only come across two of the damn things, to tell the truth. Xaphan must be a cocky son of a bitch. Of course, if I had my way, he'd soon be a dead son of a bitch, and I thought it awfully nice of him to make my job easier.

I found his coffin in the room beyond the wards, laid right out in the middle of it, as bold as you please. Most vampires make my life harder: they hide their beds, stash them away in dark corners or incredibly tight passageways. But not Xaphan. He was making this too easy. I didn't trust it.

I took my time looking around the room, searching for any wards I might have missed, trying to find the trap. No vampire was this bold, this stupid. All I found was a piece of material with an elongated diamond stitched onto it, a diamond that served as Rakkir's holy symbol. It was half- buried in the dirt floor, and I almost missed it. Though it made my stomach lurch to see it there, it wasn't booby-trapped, if it had been, I'd have been dead by now. After one more lingering look around, I decided that if humans could be so cocky they got stupid, surely vampires could too. I resolved to make his lack of security the last mistake this particular bloodsucker ever made.

I strolled over to his coffin and took a few deep breaths to steady my nerves. This was the part I hated most: opening the lid. When vampires are sleeping, nothing will wake them until nightfall. There could be an earthquake—the whole building could come down on top of them—and they wouldn't know it until night. Of course, knowing this never made me any more relaxed about lifting the lid. What if this one vampire was a light sleeper? What then? He would have the upper hand and I would soon find myself a corpse or, worse yet, turned.

So I took a deep breath, then another, building up the courage to do what I knew I must. Holding my compact out in front of me and toward the coffin, I steadied my nerves. Flipping the lid of the coffin open with one hand, I used the other to open the compact.

The dank little basement room, so dreary and dark moments before, now filled with sunlight that poured from the compact. As the beams flooded the coffin's interior with their light, an unearthly scream resounded from within the box.

Xaphan bolted out of it, flying straight up until he met the ceiling. His clothing was burning as though I'd doused him in ethanol and lit a match. His skin was charred, and obscene goo dripped off his face and fingers. He writhed there, up against the roof, screaming out his agony in an unholy voice. A drop of his oozing flesh fell upon my hand, making me jump. I kept the compact open, pointing it directly at him, watching dispassionately while he performed his grotesque dance of death upon the ceiling.

Only after the wailing stopped, when he was reduced to a revolting smell and a pile of ash that rained down all around me, did I close the compact. I pulled a bag out of my back pocket and scooped as much of his remains into it as I could. Vampires can't cross running water, so I'd toss what was left of this one into the river on my way back to see Charmaine, just in case.

As I emerged from the factory, I blinked several times to clear my vision, squinting in the bright sunlight after the shadows. Looking around, I was surprised that I didn't see Bayne or the girls. Then again, knowing him, he was busy accepting tokens of their gratitude. I guess he really was half incubus. I'd catch up with him at Llewellyn's later; right now, I needed to go see Charmaine and let her know the job was done.

My boots rang hollow on the stones as I crossed the floor, and I wondered, for the umpteenth time, if all temple designers feared being snuck up on. If not, why did they always have to make each step announce your presence so resoundingly?

She came from around the corner, moving so smoothly she seemed to float above the ground rather than walk upon it. A wide smile danced upon her lips as she saw me, standing in the middle of the great chamber in her temple of lies. Her eyes seemed to glow, maybe with delight or relief. I gazed into her eyes, mesmerized by them. If I live a hundred years, I'll never see another pair of eyes like hers.

"So you did it," she cooed, coming to within a hair's breadth of me.

"Yes. You don't need to worry about Xaphan anymore."

It felt pretty damn good to say those words, to feel as though I'd finally made up for my betrayal twenty years ago. Yeah, I was feeling pretty good—until I happened to glance down at her robe.

Where the symbol of Rakkir was usually pinned, there was ripped fabric.

Damn it!

It all made sense now. The girls hiding in the shadows, the ease with which I'd entered Xaphan's chamber, the Rakkirian symbol lying in the dirt within it. It all made sense. I looked up into Charmaine's eyes, not wanting to believe what I knew to be true.

"You've been turned."

The girls weren't hostages; they were whores playing at being held captive. No doubt they had disabled many of the traps in the factory. Charmaine didn't need me to destroy Xaphan because he threatened her girls; she needed me to get rid of competition. I'd been used, taken in, and set up using my own guilt.

I wondered, as I reached for my compact, about Bayne. Would the girls try to attack him? He could take care of himself—even taken by surprise, he would outmatch them. But how many would he be forced to slay? And how long ago had Charmaine become a vampire? Had she really been saving girls from the street all this time, or merely making them work for her? A priestess of Rakkir—who better to be a vampiric pimp than she? Surely her God was proud of her.

All these thoughts flashed through my mind as I fumbled around in my pocket, extracting the compact I thought I'd no longer needed. As I opened it, flooding the room with sunlight, only one thought remained.

Hell of a way to treat a friend.

I first met Candas when I attended one of her workshops that was spread out over several weeks. I actually signed up without knowing who the instructor was because I hoped that the deadlines would help inspire some discipline in myself. I got a whole lot more than I expected.

Candas' feedback on that novel included the words, "Your armature is showing." which so succinctly pinpointed the problem with the novel that it has entered into my personal vocabulary and is now one of the things I check for during my first editing pass. Candas has offered guidance, advice and mentorship to me in so many different ways I couldn't begin to list them all, but that was the first.

Unfortunately, that novel still isn't done (I haven't even worked on it in several years) but this short story is set in the same universe, so I think it's an appropriate contribution to this anthology.

Hopefully when Candas reads it she won't be able to spot the armature.

ANNALISE GLINKER AND ALEXANDREA
FLYNN

A LETTER FROM BEYOND

Dear Candas,

There is no word in any Earth language that can encompass all that I am, all that my people are; "overlord" is close but lacks the nuance of our full definition. Such long lives make us susceptible to insanity as early as age one hundred and thirty-seven years.

We are disguised in your world by the art of pure speculation. An art that you, your friends and your ancestors imagine you invented for yourselves; this helps my kind remain incognito. I enjoy that this missive will be safely dismissed as speculative fiction by most humans. I know that you in your intelligence are open to greater possibilities.

We've found that living half of our years among diverse host species across a variety of temporal constructs greatly prolongs our sanity, often into our nine-hundreds. We suspect that the breadth of our genius is too much for the minds of lesser species. Therefore, we avoid returning to any previous existence, to protect our own sanity and yours.

Still, I considered how I might host a life near you again but the odds of finding an intellectually compatible species and you seeking to share your home with said creature were extremely low. I have visited you and some of your companion's dreams which is how I discovered a scheme to convey thanks and tributes to you. I therefore send this artwork and letter to you via two of your friends, one of whom is a former student of yours. Appropriate proxies, I think, to show my appreciation for your lessons.

Listen to me ramble. What a wordy language you have. Let me be more direct. Communicating with anyone from a previous incarnation is highly unusual, so I must impress upon you how special you are. You may think of me as Sparrow, the name attached to the feline incarnation with which you shared some of your space and time.

In seeking various hosts, we sometimes find ourselves interacting with extremely disagreeable lesser species. When I came to you for my penultimate incarnation, my eighth life, I was impatient for my ninth life, the final life before my next transforming; a period of rest in our natural form. I had earned the right to embody a form close to my true perfection only to learn what that would mean on your world; a predator yes, but a small feline – not the apex destroyer of species as I had hoped. Your kind already had the role fully occupied. I was angry at being forced to depend on lesser bipeds and in my rage decided that your kind were no-longer worthy of our indulgence. I advocated for a clean end to humankind. We have done so to other experimental species in extreme cases. I recommended that we kick start a new evolutionary lineage – marsupials this time, perhaps, instead of primates. Then there was you.

Most humans have more faults than not but you are one of the few who inspired my kind to give your species another chance. You surprised me with the amount of patience you had for my violent outbursts and screams. Kindness over cruelty was your first lesson. A lesson that had to become a daily practice with the Pom-kind you invited into our shared home. Though I would never admit this at the time, I grew to tolerate one of the Pom-kind with something akin to kindness when compared to some of the other creatures you seem to constantly be inviting into your home. Candas, you make room for others in your life in a way that helps them make room for themselves. One of them reminded me that I could purr.

Your patience and respect for life, furry and hairless alike, and your aptitude for wonder and delight in the everyday; these were your next lessons. From the nest you made for me at your desk-side, I recall hearing your abrupt laughs or exclamations, your murmured corrections and self-explanations. I remember our shared focus on the magpies hopping about in the snow with great fondness, and the colours and patterns you surround yourself with. Everything with you is a kaleidoscope: your home, your clothes, your friends, and especially your mind.

You will see from the art piece I give to you that you are influencing me still. Did you know that I always liked the marbled paper of your hardcover books? Can you guess now my favourite colour? In my most recent life, my favourite childhood activity was spinning a toy similar to a kaleidoscope pointed at the suns. It reminds me of your warm-coloured clothes that helped me make my way to you when my eyesight was failing. I'm enjoying your artwork and I am touched by your portraits of me. Please accept this portrait as a gesture of thanks for your love, patience, respect and understanding.

As you humans say, I wish you well, may you live a long life and spin many tales. Also, congratulations on saving your species … for now.

Yours, Overlord Sparrow.

Candas was one of my instructors at Grant MacEwan. My partner, Alexandrea, and I became friends with Candas and Timothy after Candas hired Alexandrea briefly as a general Personal Assistant. The assisting was diverse including filing, yard work and painting their

house. One of the recurring tasks was cat-sitting for their elderly, and in the past, famously angry and vicious companion, Sparrow. By the time we met Sparrow she was well into her dotage and not at all vicious. The two of us regularly went for dinner with Candas and Timothy and thoroughly enjoyed spending time with them. This 'transcription' is an homage to Candas and everything that makes her a great friend and an amazing human; but especially her generosity and her delightful way of expressing her opinions and ideas. It is also an homage to a very special cat. As aspiring writers Candas has been a great source of encouragement and inspiration. Candas is also a true and dear friend.

SPRING SUNSET

That wavering fleck of dark on the other side of the river was a bat, she realised, the first of the evening. On the path to the falls, the woman paused and rested on her stick. Round her, trees and tree shadows seemed to blur and shift as sunset faded into moonrise. There was a bench ten paces behind her, but she was afraid that if she went back and sat down, she wouldn't have the will to straighten her knees again and finish the climb. Then she would have to call Armand on the intercom, and he would bring the carrier and make a fuss, and remind her of the things they could do with artificial joints these days.

But they could do things with eyes too. She could still see the bat flickering among the branches on the far side of the river. Ten years ago, even with her vodka-bottle spectacles, the scene would have been a roaring purple blur. Now she could see the loom of the moon beyond the bat, and knew that if she chose, she would be able to pick out the orange pinhead of the planet beside it. The eyes were good at seeing, all right, but like all new things, they had their deficiencies.

She started up again, moved through a net of tree shadows. The river was loud, swollen with spring. Its roar covered the creak of her breathing. A tree trunk rolled past her, and the water glittered darkly around it. Back up at the island, the bank must be crumbling. The waters were tearing away at the milestones of her life and carrying them away. She felt the new anger ache, like a life stirring within her.

Ahead, the tree reached the edge of the falls. It hung there a moment, and one of its limbs twisted into the air. Then it tilted and slid out of sight.

At the top of the path was a cleared area, with three wooden benches overlooking the falls. She intended to sit there and think until she had to go back. But when she reached the place, she was not alone.

Standing, he was taller now than she had realised, and thin. Even in those dark protective bundles, he was thin. She thought for a moment of rose bushes wrapped in sacking against the frost.

The lower part of his face was hidden by a respirator to let him breathe the air that was alien to him. His eyes were protected by lenses that caught the moonlight like silver coins.

"I thought you'd come here," he said, and though his voice came through a machine from alien flesh, it was still a young man's voice.

"I come here to be alone," she said. "You should know that. This place is full of memories. My memories."

"I wanted to be sure of finding you, before I go back finally."

"I wish you hadn't," she said. "I don't like being reminded I'm sand in an hour-glass." She leaned on her stick and coughed. "I saw another tree go over the falls just now. Every spring it happens, and they can't stop it. They can't stop things being worn away and washing over the edge."

"But something always replaces them."

"Now the replacements push their way into our lives, push us out of their way, before we're ready. And even if we resist, they get into our bodies, they change us. You don't believe in a soul, but I know—when you change a body, you change more. And they won't stop. They give us new eyes, these marvellous eyes, but they won't stop—rebuilding, always something new, always pushing—pushing."

He had not moved, but now the moonlight tilted and slid from his eyes. "It's just one modified chromosome," he said, "and some prosthetics." His voice had gone cold. "You're being melodramatic. It's just enough to let us live and breathe there. We're not a threat, we'll be too busy living our own lives, but we'll remember where we came from. We're something new, a new possibility—nothing more or less. The world has gained something through us."

"I have lost," she said, and wondered if her voice would hold. "I have lost my son."

"If you feel you have."

She stabbed her stick into the ground. "You have so much faith, don't you, in your new marvels. Let me tell you what I found out about these eyes they gave me. I found it out quite recently, something I never expected to discover. They're wonderful optical instruments— I don't doubt much better than the originals ever were. But the tear glands don't work properly. Did you know that? They don't respond to the sympathetic nervous system. That's why I can look at you now and see you clearly. Even now, like that. Like that—" Then her voice did fail her and she turned away.

Moon shadows wavered across the earth in front of her. When he moved at last, he rustled in his protective clothing like dead leaves in a wind. There was a brief touch on her shoulder, and then, after a while, the sound of leaves again, fading.

The shadows turned and darkened as the moon rose. At last she lifted her head and faced it—and the orange speck that was rising beside it. She stared at that ancient, rusty world through those marvellous eyes that would not weep, until she could imagine she saw the markings on its surface.

An owl drifted across the moon, hunting.

"Be careful," she whispered, but heard only the roar of waters.

I always associate "Spring Sunset" with Candas because I brought it to the writing workshop where I first met her, the start of a friendship

that has lasted more than thirty years. The workshop was run by the late Judith Merril for writers who had submitted to her Tesseracts *anthology. Though "Spring Sunset" wasn't critiqued there, I'd brought it along for comments because I wasn't sure if it was a story, and at one point I asked Candas to look at it. "Oh yes," she said emphatically, "it's a story." It went on to be published, and then reprinted in the anthology* Tesseracts-3, *edited by Candas and Gerry Truscott.*

A CHAT, WITH FOOTNOTES

An interview with Candas Jane Dorsey is very much like a long, lei-surely, engaging conversation with a friend—an exceptionally erudite, articulate, and intelligent friend with a huge reservoir of amusing and edifying stories. She is as generous with her ideas and memories as she was with her time as we sat in Edmonton's Café Linnea over the course of two hours, happily ensconced in the back room, amply sup-plied with food and drink.

Of course, as you've undoubtedly guessed, this interview has been edited for length and clarity and flow.

SGW: So the one thing I wanted to start with is that you're also a vis-ual artist. Is there any difference for you in creating visual art versus word art? I know you're also a poet as well as a novelist, short story writer…what else do you write?

CJD: Depending on if it's commercially or for fun, I've written pretty much the gamut of pretty much everything. I've written screenplay and I've written educational TV scripts and I've written support mate-rial for that and technical writing and computer manuals and all that kind of stuff. Lots and lots of freelance magazine journalism, mostly in the old days when there were lots of magazines. But then, also novels, short stories, poetry, essays, reviews. Good stuff.

SGW: So then maybe the question should be, is there a difference for you in creating visual art versus creative word art?

CJD: Yeah, that's a good question and there is a difference. Maybe I'll start by telling you how I got to identifying myself as a visual artist. First of all, I come from a pretty creative family and everyone in it was older than me. I was the youngest child of three and the others were 9 and 8 years older and they kind of had their turf that they had already staked out. Nobody staked out writing. My brother's a professional musician and has been an artist. My sister didn't make a living at it, but sort of approached her life as a work of art and also did a lot of visual art and stuff with her hands and so on. So I never really pursued it except as a kind of a side interest. And I was focused from a fairly early time on writing.

It's maybe even as much as ten years now, I was teaching at MacEwan and I was teaching some basic writing courses. And these young people are having to learn it as adults—which is harder, way harder because we have these language learning centres in our brain that shrink over time. So I really sympathized with their struggle, but there were large groups that I was teaching who weren't in it for writing. They were in business and so on, and they just didn't know why they should even bother. Their attitude toward precision in words was so…slipshod and they really didn't care to change it.

I had discovered the profound semi-literacy of younger readers who had been educated in the whole language approach and who have trouble reading and who have terrible trouble writing and so on. It was a real disillusionment for me and it made me wonder, who's going to read our books?

I was also at a point in my career where this was the thing I did. I used to joke to people that I did two things really well and one of them, it was illegal to charge for. {*laughs*} And the other one was the writing and editing spectrum, right? So there I was, kind of in middle age, with this thing I did that was called into question. But it was the thing I made my living in, the thing that was my image, the thing that was central to my professional life. And I was many decades from the time when I [originally] got into it because I loved the making, the creative part, right?

So part of this existential crisis was...how do I reclaim, for the next part of my life, the joy of achieving, the joy of doing the work?

The accidental answer was that I went and did a visual art...which was back at the beginning. It was back at, you're just making. You're making stuff. And you know, I'm not the same kind of visual artist as I am a writer. I'm not sort of cutting edge, way out there, whatever. I mean, I paint landscapes. So my motivation may be different, but [it] was revitalizing and it reminded me of what is was like to just be making.

I initially got into [visual art] because it didn't have a goal. You know, no sale, no display, no whatever. Just the doing. I was approaching it as an art practice.

So that's all an extremely long preamble to answer your question because they *are* different and they're different in a couple of important ways. I think one of them is I'm expressing different themes, if you will. I'm not interested in making an intellectual point with my [visual] art. If I do, it's accidental, right? But I'm mostly interested in just the ability to combine colour and shapes and give some sort of sense of how I'm seeing the world.

Shunryu Suzuki[1] talks about the spirit of repetition and about...becoming bread. In other words, he has the little parable of

---

[1] (1904–1971) Born and trained as a Soto Zen monk in Japan, Suzuki co-founded the San Francisco Zen Center in 1962.

how the Buddha made bread. To understand how ingredients became bread, he made bread over and over again. [So] we have to become bread and put ourselves into the oven. And the spirit of repetition seems to me to be a really good thing to embrace, so that's part of it.

But the other thing that I'm finding as I start to sell art is, when you write words and you sell them, you still have them. But when you make a painting and you sell it, it's gone. You can't be precious. You have to let it go and you have to believe that the next thing you do will satisfy you as much as that did.

SGW: Ok, that brings up for me the idea that even with written art, even with writing, that that piece of art is not complete until there's a reader. Just as visual art is not complete, that act—is it an act of being?—that's not complete until there are people visually experiencing it.

CJD: Some people are motivated by the need to speak, the need to be heard, or to bear witness. For me, I think if I analyze some of my writing, it's about witnessing. And about bearing witness to sometimes some pretty savage parts of the human heart or the human experience. The compulsion comes more from the sender half of the equation and there's a kind of desire to be persuasive to the receiver in terms of listening and trying not to be doctrinaire and turning people off.

I do tend to communicate these things kind of sideways...or metaphorically, but I'm not saying, what does my receiver need and then giving it to them, right? I think that is a valid process, too, and I think that a lot of writers also do. But I think it creates a slightly different kind of art.

SGW: When you're contemplating writing a new piece of something, something creative, where do you start? If it's a story, a fictional narrative, where do you usually start? Is it imagery? Character? A scene..?

CJD: All of the above, really. I have examples of all of those. What I don't usually start with is a plot. Sometimes I start with an understanding of where the journey might end, but not necessarily how to get there. If it's a short story, often it's just an impression. Or a voice of a person will suddenly pop up, or an image has come up. So over the years, [I start with] different things and sometimes [it's] just sitting down and intending to work and being open to what comes.

SGW: That's an excellent segue into my next question. Tell us a bit about your writing process. Do you have a favourite spot to write, a favourite physical location that you like to be when you're writing?

CJD: Depends on the kind of writing, but mostly I now write at my computer except poetry which I'll write in a notebook sometimes in bed {*laughs*}… because it's shorter, partly. I also have a portable, a little sort of almost-tablet that I can take to retreats or I could take out and about with me if I want to. I do end up a lot at my desk for prose writing.

SGW: And do you have a routine?

CJD: {*laughs*} No. I tell students to try and get a routine because I understand how important it is. But the reality is I have an overarching set of intentions, but they don't always translate into a daily or a weekly routine.

SGW: {*laughs*} It sounds like life. We all have an overarching set of intentions, but they don't always translate. Do you have any rituals you observe when you write?

CJD: Noo…I just try to get my butt into the chair and tell my subconscious that it's time to get moving. … You know, what's implied in that is that I really have to be careful to show up. Because life is overwhelming and making a living is overwhelming and when you make a living at the same thing, making sure that you don't get overwhelmed with one kind of thing at the expense of another, I think, is important and not always possible.

Traditionally between Christmas and New Year, we[2] do a writing retreat and we go out to Black Cat guest ranch and we have done for the last 25 years or so. Most New Years since 1991 or '92. This year we didn't because they were elsewhere. We intended to write at home, but term started so soon that I ended up doing course outlines instead. And I really really resented that. I wanted my private writing time back.

What we've done instead is last term and this, we've gotten together with a couple of other writers. We have a writing afternoon. Everybody comes to the house every week. So that's helpful. But I also have a dedicated time when I go and do visual art every week. Last term, I was teaching during that period when the group meets and I missed it. I *really* missed it. I was so glad to be back.

SGW: What I hear is you're speaking to the importance of protecting your creative time...

CJD: Yes.

SGW: ...and that what matters is to, what did you say? Get your butt in the chair. Or at your standing desk or whatever it is. Get your fingers on the keyboard and your hand wrapped around the pen.

---

[2] ref. to partner Timothy Anderson, according to Candas, a "writer, performer, and all-around Renaissance person."

CJD: Dorothea Brande[3] wrote a book called Becoming a Writer in about 1934 and she was much enamoured with the new theories about psychology and the subconscious, that were relatively new at that time. And of course, she found a lot of commonalities with writing.

One of the things she said was, [when] you make an appointment with your subconscious, you have to show up. If you don't show up, your subconscious decides you're not serious and the next time you sit down, it won't show up because you cancelled out on [the] date. So. Then you have to prove yourself and {laughs} I am so familiar with sketchy planning.

SGW: I know that you've been teaching others to write for many years and you are a mentor for many writers, especially in the area of speculative fiction, but I'm sure just generally in creative writing. So in addition to "Show up"—make a date with your subconscious and show up—what would be two other pieces of advice that you've found yourself giving to the writers that you've mentored and taught?

CJD: Well, one is to finish things. Because finishing is a fraught process. Starting is a fraught process, but as long as you've started, you can say, well I've written. At some point, you have to finish and hand it over to the receiver and complete the feedback loop.

I do talk to students about co-creation and how the reader co-creates the story and so on. Part of that is, they have to have something to look at, you know. Even if it's not good. You can always fix it, right? So that's another part of the message: don't worry at first about perfection. Worry about getting it done.

I also learned in early years from a variety of teachers, some of whom were nurturing. And then there was Rudy Wiebe. {laughs wryly} I think he's wonderful actually for what he's done for the world,

---

[3] (1893–1948) Brande was an American writer and editor, also famous for her 1936 inspirational book, Wake Up and Live!

but I also understand that he was the kind of teacher who believed in tough love. I think as many people as responded to that, say Aritha Van Herk or Scot Morrison or I, there were also the people who found it bruising at an early part of their career.

My decision as a teacher is to let the actual writing world bruise people, as it does, rather than taking an active role in the bruising process. So I encourage people and I let them know: This is hard. It's going to be hard. You're gonna have hard things to do. You're gonna discover that you don't know stuff that you really need to know. That's okay. Just get stuff done and then learn how to assess your stuff and then try for the highest level of excellence.

We know more now about what's called the Dunning-Kruger Effect[4]. To put it in pop culture terms: stupid people think they're smart. At the the other end of the spectrum, smart people judge themselves more highly...because they *do* know the complexities of the task. But what I just discovered recently that is also part of Dunning and Kruger's findings is, when you know a task really well, you then begin to think it's easy. Trying to convey to others how to do it, you gloss over the difficult things because you've internalized them.

So there's a whole process involved in, how do you learn how to distinguish between good and bad in your writing and then not be bad? Which is difficult. And then, how do you maintain high standards while not being dismissive about how difficult it is? As a teacher of writing and a mentor, those things concern me.

There's another piece of research about music[5]. Somebody did brain scans of people listening to music. They found that [when listening to music,] people who knew nothing about music listened with a different part of their brain than people who had an extensive musical

---

[4] Named for David Dunning and Justin Kruger of Cornell Unversity, whose experiments resulted in a 1999 paper entitled, "Unskilled and unaware of it: how difficulties in recognizing one's own incompetence lead to inflated self-assessments."

[5] To find just one example of this research, google "Sting's brain on music."

education and experience. I heard a composer talking about this on CBC and what he was basically saying was, what that means is that after you're composing for a while, you're composing for other composers.

So part of teaching and mentoring is to retain a part of your brain that has the innocence that remembers how hard things were and also how clueless one is at the beginning, and then trying to sort of shine the light on the path through that dark forest.

Someone once described the ideal workshop process as *vicious but fair*. I wouldn't say vicious, but, certainly, you can be exacting and still be compassionate, still be empathic.

SGW: It's interesting that the farther one is in one's practice, the easier it is to forget that your own standards are changing.

CJD: Yes...and you know, people mentored me. And taught me, including Rudy[Wiebe], and taught me invaluable lessons sometimes with a single word or a single moment. and I think it's important to be part of an historical process and pass that on.

SGW: Speaking of mentorship, what do you think is the top pitfall for people who are mentors regarding their mentees?

CJD: Well, there are a couple of pitfalls. One of them is you use all your creative energies helping other people be creative. Using up one's creative energy helping others achieve, this isn't a bad thing. But it's a thing to be aware of and set boundaries. And the other one is...you get Stockholm Syndrome and begin to lose your absolute standards. You know, you waiver between compassion and quality.

SGW: So, as a mentee, how does one find their mentor and/or what should one reasonably expect from one's mentor?

CJD: From my experience, you find your mentor by going to where the work is and take a look at who's been doing it for a long time or who's doing it. This sounds simple, but there's a...kind of modern point of view that says confidence and enthusiasm are enough.

SGW: {*laughs*}

CJD: {*chuckles*} Someone was talking about women in politics getting young men mansplaining to them. She posted a cartoon, I think probably a New Yorker, that said, let me overwhelm your experience with my confidence, kind of thing, right? So, you know, people of a certain amount of experience understand that other people's experience can be deeply instructive. People who don't have a lot of experience sometimes get the experience version of the Dunning-Kruger Effect and they think they've got it all down. There's an old joke, I think it was Mark Twain, though he gets everything attributed to him, but...he said that when he came home from college, he was amazed at how much his father had learned in four years. We're all a bit like that.

Be prepared to let [your mentor] know and to thank them and maybe sometimes to offer them something in return because you are truly being given a gift when people give you their time and their expertise. It's a gift.

I try to send every class off to be a writing group on their own and I try to make them not dependent on me.

SGW: That would be the number one job of a mentor.

CJD: Yeah. I'm not interested in the cult of personality. Being a sycophant or being a supporter of a personality is not a mentorship relationship. So I say this to [my students] and they're kind of taken aback in a way.

I remember this moment, it was not long after my dad died, it was in '97. Death is difficult to process and I walked into this classroom [to] this group of students and I had one of those moments. I thought, all I really want to say to these people is, what are you doing here? Go home and write. Then, a split second later, realizing, but they don't know what they need to know yet to be able to just go home and do that.

So my reason for being hasn't changed, but my attitude to it changed and I actually, as a result of that little moment, changed my teaching practice. I would be more transparent about my desire to disattach them from their unequal relationship, unequal power relationship. Several pretty solid groups have carried on from classes that I've done. That's not direct mentorship, but it is sort of saying, ok you're empowered now. Here's some tools. Go do stuff.

SGW: I would respectfully disagree. That is mentorship. You're setting up people for a succesful practice. Whether it *is* succesful or a regular practice, is up to them, as it should be. You've empowered them to make that choice for themselves. ...You know, humbly, I submit.

CJD: {*laughs*} I will accept.

SGW: You've given us some pieces of advice about writing. What has been for you the best piece of advice about writing that you have received and by whom was it given?

CJD: I don't know if I can give you *the* best, but I can give you a few. ... W.O. Mitchell basically said, Don't quit. That was his advice. Every time he saw me, that's what he would say first. He'd hug me and he'd say, You didn't quit. Kid, you didn't quit. But he also said things like, sit down and type everyday. He called it Mitchell's Messy Method. It was basically free fall: get your butt in the seat and do stuff. But his big thing was, don't quit.

Rudy [Wiebe] made people be good at it. He was not interested in people who perceived the activity as trivial or a hobby or something. He wanted people to be good at it and he wanted that in a very stern, strict, Mennonite kind of way. I remember once he stood in front of about 200 people at the Writers' Guild [of Alberta], who'd asked him to be a speaker and he basically said, of all of you 200 people in this room, only 2 of you will ever make it. {*laughs*} Like, thanks a lot. He didn't intend to be as mean as it sounds. What he intended to say was, You gotta take yourself seriously and you gotta produce. You gotta pony up and you gotta do it right.

I had a mentor in my childcare work who said, one time when I worried about whether someone I worked with liked me, she said, would you like Hitler to approve of you? And that was pretty powerful learning and I've applied that many times.

SGW: In terms of being a person but also in terms of being an artist and wanting everybody to love you—

CJD: Yeah, you can't and so you end up choosing your enemies. You choose what and ...{*chuckles*} I still haven't finished the other question and now I have a new thing I want to talk about.

SGW: {*laughs*} This is a freeform conversation.

CJD: So, when I was first freelancing I spent a weekend travelling around with Judy Chicago[6], the artist who did the Dinner Party Project, among other things. At one point, we were in Saskatoon with the group of women who started the Shoestring Gallery which was a fem-

---

[6] (b. July 20, 1939) Chicago is an American feminist artist, art educator, and writer.

inist gallery collective. This was about 1981, somewhere in there. I was writing about it for the Visual Arts Newsletter. We're walking into this house where this meeting is and I said to Chicago, I really envy you this sense of community these women have because where I'm at in the writing community, there isn't that much sort of solid community for us. She just looked at me and she said, Make it. Then she walked into the house.

Two words, changed everything about my life, right? Because all the community building stuff that I've done was partly for others and it was partly for me. To have a community, to have people who are in the same boat. ... You know, so that was a moment all right 'cause she didn't waste any words. She was amazing.

Around the same time, a group of us got together and we brought Jane Rule[7] to Edmonton to do some events. She was the one who said, and also changed the way I looked at the world, Politics is housework.

When you're young and you think you can change the world, you think you're gonna change it and it's gonna stayed changed. Then it doesn't work and then you get soured and disillusioned and you become a disillusioned activist who then gets really grouchy about how none of this is possible and possibly turns right-wing like Barbara Amiel[8] or becomes a naysayer. [Rule's comment] stopped that. Because ok, it's housework.

SGW: It's never done.

CJD: {*nods*} Judy Merril[9] of course was a good friend and a good mentor and someone I deeply admired. I just think I've been really

---

[7] (1931–2007) From the NY Times: "...a prominent Canadian writer whose first novel, 'Desert of the Heart,' is considered a landmark work of lesbian fiction."

[8] (b. Dec. 4, 1940) British-Canadian journalist and socialite known for right-wing views.

[9] (1923–1997) Pen name of Judith Grossman, an American/Canadian writer known as "the little mother of science fiction" and who founded the Merril Col-

fortunate in whom I've been able to meet. Judy and I once had sushi dinner with Ursula and Charles Le Guin in Toronto and then they paid for it, so {*chuckles*} peak experience number 1, 2, and 3 all in one night.

SGW: You mentioned a couple of people involved specifically in what we broadly call "speculative fiction." What do you think spec fic has to offer for readers and writers that is different than other genres have to offer?

CJD: {*long pause*} Allegory. The secret is that all fiction is speculative anyway because none of it happened. Samuel Delaney made that point. He said, anything that happens in a realistic story can happen in a science fiction story, but not the other way around. So which one is the subset of which, right?

One evening at the Milford-style workshop Judith Merril organised in Peterborough, Ontario, in 1986, which was dubbed SFWorkshop Canada Ink... [Judith] invited the writers who had been included in the first Tesseracts anthology, which she had edited the year before and launched at Harbourfront (Reading Series). Eight writers (and three significant others) attended. [That night,] Judy Merril and Terry Green[10] were talking about how this field [spec fic] was about to go through a growth spurt and talking about the terms. Damon Knight[11] once said that science fiction is what you're pointing to when you use the term. And people would say, well what is fantasy, what is science fiction, what is SFF?

---

lection of Science Fiction, Speculation & Fantasy, housed within the Toronto Public Library.

[10] (b. Feb. 2, 1947) Canadian science fiction and fantasy writer, Terence M. Green.

[11] (1922–2002) American writer and editor of science fiction, whose short story, "To Serve Man" was adapted into an episode of The Twilight Zone.

We literally decided in that room that we were gonna go out from there and say, we're gonna call it speculative fiction in Canada to cover all the bases because there were Francophone writers writing everything from hard SF to *la fantastique*, which is a different tradition in French. Plus the Anglophone writers writing SF, fantasy in both genre and literary terms, magic realism, horror and so on. And it was all going to be part of the inclusive term, speculative fiction.

It wasn't a new term, of course, but we decided it was going to be the Canadian descriptive term from that day on! I mean, other people had talked about it. Seems to me it was a term that Theodore Sturgeon[12] and Judy [Merril] had liked to use in the fifties and Hank Hargreaves[13] did a whole series of radio shows from Edmonton in the sixties in which he used that term and tried to popularize it. So it wasn't new, but it was such a good blanket terminology for a whole lot of stuff that people do. Critically, as well as market-wise, we wanted it to be clear that there was a Canadian version. So naming it a thing, we felt, was important. Which probably also came from Delaney: what you call a thing then determines how people think about it.

But to go back to the question of allegory. So many of our early tales and our early narratives in humanity are about trying to explain reality by allegory or trying to get people to learn how to behave better through allegory. My core argument is that you can do stealth work with speculative fiction because you can, by using allegorical things, abstract them from people's known context—and then you can make them think about them without getting defensive. If you say, you or your neighbour might be a child abuser, people're gonna say, am not, or, is not. But if you say, here's a thing that happens on a planet, and then make them think about how humans behave with each other in the here and now, then you've accomplished the allegorical

---

[12] (1918–1985) American editor and writer of science fiction, fantasy, and horror.

[13] (1928–2017) Canadian science fiction writer, H.A. Hargreaves.

task that narrative does. And you've gotten further, you've dug in deeper, you've gotten under their radar. You've gotten past their defences, so it's a very powerful tool.

SGW: Does this mean that you don't particularly care for hyper-realistic narratives?

CJD: It doesn't matter if they're hyper-realistic. They're not real life. It's like hyper-realism in painting, right? It still abstracts the world and presents it a certain way. It's a choice about how the world will be seen by the person who makes the art.

I want to talk about John Clute's theory of fantasy which is in The Encyclopedia of Fantasy[14] and I give it out to all my writing classes whether they write fantasy or not. Because [Clute] talks about what he calls a self-completing narrative. He talks about a narrative, a story—he specifically uses the word "story"—in terms of a process that starts with establishment of wrongness, of something, of a note that is wrong. Something strikes wrongly. [It] proceeds through a progressive thinning of the nature of the known world, to a point where, as he so beautifully puts it, the protagonist looks at the shrivelled heart of the thinned world and knows what to do. And then, action takes place. Something is done, it works or it doesn't work, and there's a resolution that ends the story by pressing forward into, in essence, outcomes. Tolkien called it consolation. Clute calls it, sometimes, healing, but it's not always positive, right? But it's an outcome. He says that at the point at which an action takes place, [it] becomes a story that can be completed by its protagonist and so on.

So he says stories that get stuck in wrongness, that describes supernatural fiction: things are not real. Things are not as they are. Then, he says, [the] horror [narrative] is stuck in thinning. Various types of fantasy require the completion of the quest, or the return to just gov-

---

[14] c. 1997. Edited by John Clute and John Grant.

ernance: the king, the land heals, there's marriage, there's whatever whatever. Think about a romance novel, right? Things are wrong somehow. Things get worse, there's thinning. But at some point, the protagonist, even in the most genre novel, is gonna be going through this process of, in essence, some sort of natural justice, pointing out who she's supposed to be with, or he, and they get to live happily ever after, right?

So the difficulty I have is that {*long pause*} mainstream literature doesn't think of itself as a genre. But it *is* a genre. I look at the sort of classic CanLit or the classic MFA short story, and what I see is a narrative that is stuck in either wrongness or thinning. Which is exactly the same as what happens in supernatural fictions or horror. Except it's happening with intentions in realism. But you take a set of unsavoury characters often already with several strikes against them in the game of life, and you stick them in their unhappy lives. Usually, there's a child at risk or there's a pet at risk or there's a dead gerbil or some damned thing, right? And you don't ever let them move through their story, even in a novel.

You know, I'm reading along happily in a mainstream novel and it just sort of stops. It stops before it gives you enough data to even guess the outcome. So then you realize you're not *supposed* to know the outcome and all this is supposed to do is to make you feel a certain way for a hundred sixty or three hundred and sixty pages. Or, you know, in terms of the short story, it gives you a hit of the wrongness without ever giving you any tools to say anything is possible [or] even [that] an unhappy ending is possible.

I'm afraid that this does bother me and pisses me off. Because I think our narratives in life, they don't necessarily resolve the way we want them, but they progress. They're progressing. and to take too narrow a snapshot is very, I think, judgmental. I truly think that it, that the people who write these stories don't understand that what they're doing is they're speaking from a place of privilege to say, I am better than you because I see that your life is hopeless and shitty.

I'm not interested in that. I mean, I do write about some pretty difficult lives, but there is always somewhere in me a sense that progression of some sort is possible. Progress through to, at least, new understanding, if not to a happier place to live in after—or to joy or whatever. At least, *understand* that it's possible. Also, I just don't feel all that hierarchically better or more interesting than my characters are.

I had this argument when I was…. I took an MFA late in life, partly because I wanted to regularize my teaching credentials and partly because I was interested in exploring certain areas that I just hadn't had the leisure to do. One of the courses I took was a creative non-fiction course. Now, I'd written stuff like it and was writing a book at the time. I've since kind of abandoned it. {*chuckles*} I discovered that someone else wrote it way better.

I wasn't actually allowed to work on that book [in my MFA course] even though that's where I was at with my creative non-fiction. I had to do a personal essay, and I'm… {*smiles*} I'm not exactly biddable sometimes and I basically got a little contumacious and I said, I'm not at the point in my career where I had to practice these things. I'm at a point where I'm actually trying to improve my mastery in a certain area, but I have ideas, I said, and my ideas are interesting, but *I'm* not that interesting. In terms of my out-there-in-the-world and writing this sort of classic *me* essay, *me* journalism…I'm not what's most interesting about what I want to write. I want to write about characters and situations and ideas that I'm capable of thinking of that are interesting.

Of course, that was not an argument that really washed. So I sort of contumaciously wrote the wrong essays.

I was supposed to write an essay about a person who'd been important to me, so I wrote about all the dead bodies I'd seen and who they were and what was the situation and so on. I was supposed to write a nature essay, so I wrote one called Why I Hate Nature. And oh, a place that had been important to me. I forget what I did… .

The instructor, at the end of the course, actually shifted them around. He said, you didn't do what I said in any of the three assignments, but you did them in one of the other assignments, so I'm gonna shift it and make that one your personal essay and that one your whatever. And then I can give you marks because otherwise I'll have to mark you zero.

So. I wrote a whole bunch of stuff, but it was zero because it didn't fit.

Clearly, that's what I feel about genres. People have to write what they are most passionate about. They have to. Because writing is hard and if you don't write what you love, you're gonna lose your energy and you're never gonna finish anything.

You know, I set out once to write a romance novel 'cause I thought I could make my fortune. I couldn't get four pages into it because that wasn't what I'm passionate about. It's not what I read. It wasn't how I perceived the natural justice of the universe to work its way out, right? I didn't see people's ultimate outcome to settle down and live happily and bear children in suburbia or whatever. That didn't mean it was bad and, in fact, that gave me a huge amount more respect for romance as a genre because a person who doesn't love any genre can't really write it. Like, they can write it competently and they can maybe even sell it. They can maybe go to the bank and maybe they can even set up their pension plan on it, but that doesn't mean that it's gonna hit their heart.

SGW: {*speaks over last 6 words*} But there's no soul.

CJD: Yeah. There are some people who like to not be challenged by what they read. They're reading the same way that they're eating burgers. That means that there's a place for burger-flipping cooks as well as a place for gourmet cooks. I have less and less to say about the difference between those two food stuffs. {*smiles*} The older I get, the more burgers I eat.

Whatever you love to do, you've gotta do it. Otherwise, you can't get the energy together to weather the difficulties, the learning how to do it right. The fact that you might not get published. The fact that even if you do get published, you won't make any money. The things you have to do to make money so that you can do your writing. All those things are hard work and you've gotta want to be fuelled by true, deep motivation, passion, anger…

I consider a lot of my writing to be fuelled, in fact, by anger. At the things that I found out during that very short time when I was a child care worker. At the injustices of the world—ongoing, but also the ones that I became aware of when I was sort of coming of age in my early 20s. And that fuel has been stoking the boilers ever since. As it should be. Anger is not rage. Anger is a nice pure clean flame. But other kinds of passion too; the passion to have fun and to laugh that fuels comedy.

Neil Gaiman wrote about a conversation[15] he had with Pratchett where Pratchett said, you have no idea how much anger I have, and what I write is fuelled by my anger.

Look at what [Pratchett] wrote about and how he wrote it and how he used comedy and fantasy to achieve these really heavy duty goals, right? [It] is specifically fascinating because Pratchett was so smart and he knew what was driving him and it wasn't jolly, you know? The humour was necessary, I think, because if you don't laugh, you die.

Especially when you look at the world, you have a choice. Do you feel horrified and stay in the basement in the hope that the current president of the United States doesn't immolate us all with nuclear weapons? Or, do you laugh and…retweet the latest joke kind of thing? Frankly, I think that people who are able to laugh have more ability to perceive ironies and have more ability to let allegory get them and so…{*smiles*} that was kind of a rant, but that really is where I'm coming from.

---

[15] as published in The Guardian, Sept. 24, 2014.

I learned to say to writing students, Don't practice. You're at the beginning of your career and you think, oh I should practice on something harmless, right? It's the equivalent of giving injections to oranges and grapefruit instead of to actual human beings when you're first practising.

But at a certain point, and for a writer, it's fairly early, you really have to quit practising and start writing what you care about. Even if you write it badly, you can always fix it. Or you can write it again. If you really care about it, you're gonna write it over and over anyway in different forms. So just do it because practising wastes your time.

It takes as much time to write a bad book as it takes to write a good book. It does. So try to write a good book at the very beginning and also understand that sometimes you gotta write it bad in order to write it good later. Not just write it badly, but let it be bad. And then, let it get good by learning.

People ask me too about...political correctness, basically. In the broadest sense of what I'm talking about. You draft something, it's full of all your prejudices and weirdnesses. It's full of fast typing and it's full of the things that you learned when you were 6 or whatever. But at the point where you've finished typing the first draft, you are not done.

And one of the times you look at that draft, you have to look at it and say, is it on the right side of history? Can I stand behind this? Twenty or 30 or 40 years from now, when it's sitting on a shelf and someone rereads it, do I want them to say, oh my gosh, that was so dated, and look at how wooden those characters are and look at all those little speeches they make and about this and that and how this must've hit the right point in history to even get published? Or, do you want them to say, it holds up. It holds up because it's authentic. Because it still has something to say about the human predicament.

One of the things we're responsible to do is to look at [our work] and make sure it's not racist. Look at it and make sure it's not sexist. Look at it and make sure it's not homophobic. We can't put the brakes on our first-draft selves, but part of our responsibility is to make sure our first-draft self is not someone we're ashamed of when we go out in public. I mean, unless we're really socially inept, none of us scratches our private parts while we're standing in front of a crowd of people giving a speech, right? I mean, that's what we learned. We learned to make ourselves presentable without negating who we are.

I think it's incumbent on us as writers to learn how to be better people. And {*chuckles*} it's not just idealistic. It means less typing. It really does. And I'm all for less typing. I hate typing. I'm not a typist.

So you wanna eliminate the things that make it harder to write. So use your tools, but also, some of your tools are yourself. So eliminate the pieces that you know are crappy. Get it so that it's second nature not to make certain slurs or use certain words. And it's the same as getting it so that it's second nature to know the difference between *lie* and *lay*. Or to not put apostrophes in the possessive *its*. If people give themselves permission to be sloppy like that, it just wastes their time later.

SGW: So, we're kind of wrapping up now. What's been the most surprising aspect of your career so far, as an artist? Or would you like to expand that to community organizer, activist? However you'd like to.

CJD: Surprising in a good way, is probably discovering that the visual art is an option and a practice.

Some of the surprises aren't as happy. I think rediscovering sexism as I got older. Rediscovering that I was gonna have to battle, and listening to young women have the same battles as 40 years ago. That was a bit of a surprise. Discovering that the whole language approach in teaching for the last 30 and 40 years has created a generation (or several) of people who don't know their own language. [That] was an unfortunate surprise.

{*Laughs*} On some level, it's all been a surprise. I mean, I never had a plan. I did what I did and there would be a plan in the short term and maybe a few years, but it wasn't like, you're gonna do this and these things will ensue. I realized that part of why I'm surprised at things is 'cause I didn't expect anything, you know. And sometimes the negative surprises are because I expected some *thing*.

All the cool stuff that's happened and just the people that I've had a chance to meet and places I've had a chance to go as well as just looking at some of the reactions. I think I was truly and utterly and completely surprised by the Prairie Starport project. There was nothing telegraphed and Rhonda sent me this message and I'm just sitting at my desk, going {*laughs*}. That was a big surprise. And I'm not just saying that .... You know, some of the recognitions[16] that I've received were [a surprise] 'cause you never know if it's really working, what you're trying to do, especially in community work. You really never know. If it works, then you see it. That's so cool.

SGW: What's something you're still aspiring toward?

CJD: To get the almost four books that I've written and never got published, published. To make the latter part of my life have as much meaning as the other parts did, which is not always easy. When the world and entropy take things away from you, to continue to feel like you're a builder or that you're moving forward, is a choice rather than an accident at that point. To not end up eating cat food in a rooming house. {*laughs*} The problem with, you know, *follow your bliss and the money will follow*, is that the money doesn't actually follow. Yeah, you gotta have a back up plan.

SGW: This is my last question and you can take your time with it. Describe a perfect day for you.

---

[16] Most recently, Candas received the 2017 Writers' Guild of Alberta Golden Pen Award for lifetime achievement by an Alberta writer.

CJD: A perfect day is a day when ... I'm not anxious about money or the fate of some historic site or {*laughs*} whether some idiot's finger is on the nuclear button or whatever. Where I'm actually free to do my work and to have sort of some rewarding relationships and I don't feel like I'm getting distracted by earning a living or fussing about something or requirements that come from outside myself.

I think I haven't been good at setting boundaries at some periods in my life between the community service person, the family obligations person, and the writer person. I think that is something that some people are able to do and are able to be very single-minded about their artistic careers and I never was. I still yearn for a little bit more single-mindedness.

So that's another thing I aspire to...is to actually continue to give myself permission to be first and foremost the writer, the artist, the creator, and not have to earn my keep. Because I think...I come from some Scots Presbyterian heritage and really, literally, people were told they had to earn their keep, in those words. So there's this implication that you have to earn your right to just be. And, especially as a creative person, is that real work? And it takes people years to process that yeah, it's real work and it's art. And then you keep backsliding on that.

So, a perfect day is a day when I get to write or make art, you know, and do what I do in a community of other people and don't have to worry about the Sword of Damocles {*laughs*}, whatever form it might take, I guess.

Oh and I get to eat sushi. {*big laugh*} Don't forget sushi!

ABOUT CANDAS

Candas Jane Dorsey is the internationally-known, award-winning author of novels *Black Wine* (originally Tor, re-released Five Rivers) and *Paradigm of Earth* (Tor); short story collections *Machine Sex and other stories, Dark Earth Dreams, Vanilla and other stories* and *ICE and other stories*; four poetry books; several anthologies edited/co-edited, and numerous published stories, poems, reviews, and critical essays. She was the editor/publisher for fourteen years of the literary press The Books Collective, including River Books and Tesseract Books. She teaches writing to adults and youth, communications at MacEwan University, and speaks widely on SF and other topics. She was founding president of SFCanada, and has been president of the Writers Guild of Alberta. In 2005 she was awarded the Province of Alberta Centennial Gold Medal for her artistic achievement and community work, and in 2017 the WGA Golden Pen Award for Lifetime Achievement in the Literary Arts. She is also a community activist, advocate and leader.

ACKNOWLEDGEMENTS

"Slough" by Timothy J. Anderson is original to this anthology.

"The Smut Story" by Greg Bechtel was originally published in Boundary Problems (Freehand, 2014) and is reprinted by permission of Freehand books.

"Candas of Boyle Street" by Anita Jenkins is original to this anthology.

"Good Eating" by Gregg Chamberlain was originally published by Daily Science Fiction.

"Jimmy Smith Has a Dinosaur" by Gregg Chamberlain was originally published by Daily Science Fiction.

"Afternoon Break" by Gregg Chamberlain was originally published by Daily Science Fiction.

"Sami's Song" by Laina Kelly is original to this anthology.

"About Candas" by Barb Galler-Smith is original to this anthology.

"The Secret of Freedom" by BD Wilson is original to this anthology.

"One Day I'm Going to Give Up The Blues For Good" by Ursula Pflug was originally published in Prairie Fire Vol. 15, No. 2, 1994.

"Avoidance" by Eileen Bell was originally published on CBC's "Alberta Anthology".

"Father Time" by Derryl Murphy was originally published in *Tesseracts 4* edited by Lorna Toolis and Michael Skeet, 1992.

"Split Decision" by Robert Runté was originally published in *Tesseracts Fifteen: A Case of Quite Curious Tales* edited by Julie Czerneda and Susan MacGregor, 2011; and reprinted in Imaginarium 2012: The Best Canadian Speculative Writing edited by Sandra Kasturi and Halli Villegas, 2012.

"Candas Jane Dorsey: A Friendship Spanning 40+ Years" by Diane L. Walton is original to this anthology.

"Sister Margaret" by Rhonda Parrish was originally published by Wild Child Publishing in 2006.

"A Letter From Beyond" by Annalise Glinker and Alexandra Flynn is original to this anthology. The accompanying art, "Overlord Sparrow" is also original to this anthology.

"Spring Sunset" by John Park was originally published by in *On Spec* 2(1) in 1990.

"A Chat, with Footnotes: S.G. Wong Interviews Candas Jane Dorsey" is original to this anthology.

www.ingramcontent.com/pod-product-compliance
Lightning Source LLC
Chambersburg PA
CBHW022151240626
47153CB00007B/2610